Hannah's Winter

Kierin Meehan

Kane Miller

A DIVISION OF EDC PUBLISHING

Kane/Miller Book Publishers, Inc.
First American Edition 2009
by Kane/Miller Book Publishers, Inc.
La Jolla, California

Copyright © Kierin Meehan, 2001
Originally published by Penguin Group (Australia), 2001

Library of Congress Control Number: 2008932432
Printed and bound in China by Regent Publishing Services, Ltd.
2 3 4 5 6 7 8 9 10

ISBN: 978-1-933605-98-2

For Patrick Alphonsus and Ada Sarah

If you, finder, choose to help the ocean boy,
Wait for the first snowfall.
The flute player at the temple of secrets
has the fox light.
At the hour of the bull bring the light to the shrine
Where women go to poison the hearts of their rivals.
After the bean throwing
Take the talisman you receive
To the place where the old mountain god
waits in the forest.
With the gift and your winter words from
the house of cards
Go at sunrise to wake the dragon that
sleeps in the lord's garden.
But beware the one
Who does not want the boy to go.
And remember always:
Blue for safety, yellow is warning, red means danger.

Chapter One

I met the Maekawas on a Saturday late in January. My mother brought me to their house in a pale-green taxi. We arrived three hours before they expected us because of the sign on the wall of our Osaka hotel room:

WE HOPE WE CAN SERVE YOU WITH HEARTY AND TENDER SERVICE AND BE LOVED BY YOU ALL.
NO LAUNDRY SERVICE SATURDAY OR SUNDAY.
SIGNED: THE GENERAL MANAGER.

I woke to find my mother glaring at it.

"If he wants to be loved," she said, "he should offer a weekend laundry service. We'll have to catch an early train so I can do my washing in Kanazawa. I can't travel again tomorrow without doing my washing. Get up IMMEDIATELY, Hannah."

We arrived at Kanazawa Station on the train from Osaka at about three o'clock. Rain was spattering down out of a bleak sky and we were chilled to the bone standing in the taxi queue. Our mountains of luggage, piled up around us like building blocks, and my mother's purple hair, were attracting a lot of the wrong kind of attention. I could see that none of the taxi drivers wanted us as passengers. The one who got stuck with us looked as if he couldn't believe his bad luck. Actually, he probably thought I was okay. But a look of pure horror crossed his face as my mother stalked towards him in her spiky, black boots and leopard-print coat, hair iridescent against the grey winter sky.

He didn't talk to us in the taxi because he was watching TV! He had a mini TV set built into his dashboard and every time we stopped at a red light his head would bob to the left and down so he could watch. What a great idea! I kept one eye on the TV and watched Kanazawa roll past with the other. Through the splintery rain I saw grey buildings, grey streets, cars, umbrellas, bare trees.

My mother had come to Japan to research her new book, a coffee table book called *Surprising Japanese Gardeners*. I told her it should be called *Surprised Japanese Gardeners* because they'd be very surprised after they'd met her. My mother ignores me when I say things like that. She's a horticulturist. She writes "This Month's Gardening Tips" for a magazine called *Fascinating Australian Gardens* and sometimes she appears on television on daytime talk shows. Bert Newton will ask her how to grow perfect winter pansies, or Rick Burnett on "Brisbane Extra" will say, "Next, Liana Forrester's going to tell us about an herb that may cure your varicose veins." Liana, that's her name, and a tough old rainforest vine she is too.

TV was how she got purple hair. She did an interview on "Brisbane Extra" about jacarandas in November last year, so she dyed her hair the same color as the jacaranda flowers, for fun. Afterwards she decided purple suited her personality, so she'd keep it that way for a while. She's like a runaway horse when she gets an idea in her head. Uncontrollable. That's how I ended up in Kanazawa.

She insisted on bringing me to Japan, even though I didn't want to come. It would have been logical to leave me behind. After all, she'd be traveling most of the time. First she was going to Tokyo to interview a bonsai master, then north to Hokkaido to look at farms and vegetable plots, and south to Okinawa, where she'd heard of a housewife who'd created a tropical wilderness on the balcony of her apartment. And then on again, to landscape gardens and moss gardens and Zen gardens. I couldn't travel with her – "It'll be RUSH, RUSH, RUSH, Hannah, you'd never keep up" – so she had to find somewhere in Japan for me to live.

I wanted to stay home in Brisbane with my dad and my older brother, Joel. Well, I didn't really want to stay with Joel.

Nobody would. He's gross. But Dad and me, that would have been fun. Dad's a laid-back, drifty, dreamy soul. My mother says it's because he was born in Tasmania. And because he's artistic. With Dad in charge I could have had three months of videos and takeout food and nobody making a fuss about homework. And I would have started high school with my friends, at the end of January when I was supposed to.

But if it's logical my mother won't do it. She's opposed to logic and common sense. If there were street marches protesting against logic, she'd be at the front of the crowd carrying the biggest banner.

"I won't have any arguments, Hannah. You ARE coming with me. It won't hurt you to miss the first few months of high school. They'll only be reviewing Year Seven work and having silly barbecues until April. Living in Japan will be a WONDERFUL experience for you. You can stay in Kanazawa with my friend Kie and her family. Her daughter Mikiko – they call her Miki – is about a year older than you. Kie's husband runs a stationery shop. And he's a *washi* collector!"

"You mean he collects bits of paper?"

"No, Hannah, don't be dim. He collects Japanese paper goods, anything pretty or unusual or old. He has kites and parasols and fans, paper dolls, masks and old books, all jumbled together in the Old Corner of his shop. Quite lovely and SO educational, but they DO collect a LOT of dust! You'll ADORE it! The paper, not the dust. And just think how FLUENT your Japanese will be by the time you come

4

back. Besides, if you stay behind with your father, he'll let you get away with MURDER."

My mother talks in capitals when she's being assertive, which is most of the time.

I suspect she guessed that getting away with murder was my motivation for staying home, because learning Japanese was never a reason for me to go with her. I already spoke Japanese well. Dad worked for a Tokyo design company for two years when I was little, and I went to preschool there. And I'd been learning Japanese at primary school since the beginning of Year Five. I was the top Japanese student in Year Seven at Opal Street State School. Actually, I was top in most subjects but I won't go on about that. My mother says it GETS ON PEOPLE'S NERVES.

The problem, the one in my mother's purple head, was that I couldn't read Japanese well, or write it. If you've ever learned Japanese or known someone who has, you'll know there are three scripts – *hiragana, katakana,* and *kanji*. I was a whiz at the first two: they've only got forty-six symbols each. But I didn't know many *kanji* and that was my mother's gripe. Her plan was for me to learn at least one thousand *kanji* during the three months we'd be in Japan. She didn't explain how this miracle was to happen.

"It's the MINIMUM number you should know, Hannah. Japanese children learn ONE THOUSAND *kanji* in PRIMARY school."

That's how I ended up outside Miki's house, which was

also the Maekawas' shop, on a January afternoon. My suitcases were bulging with gifts. I had chocolate macadamias, three I LOVE OZ shirts, four Australian wildflower coffee mugs, a rainforest calendar, a CD of didgeridoo music and a toothpick holder shaped like a crocodile. Then there were tracksuits and woolen socks and tights and sweaters and gloves for the cold weather, as well as a brown envelope of correspondence lessons. Did I mention that? In my spare time, when I wasn't absorbing enormous numbers of *kanji*, I was supposed to be starting Year Eight by correspondence. Another of my mother's IDEAS.

The Maekawas' home had two entrances – one through their shop, the other from a narrow lane at the back of the house, through a small garden. Our driver pulled up in front of the shop. At the same moment, a white delivery van trundled around the corner. The automatic door of the taxi swung open and my mother and I scrambled out just as the van driver pulled up nose-to-nose with the taxi.

"Here we are, Hannah. This is the Mulberry Tree."

I looked at the little brown shop. Its sliding doors were shut. Blue and white *noren* curtains hung across them.

"The Mulberry Tree? That's a weird name for a stationery shop." Did the Maekawas sell preserved fruits or jams on the side? I stepped sideways in a hurry as our taxi driver almost dumped a suitcase on my foot.

"It's quite logical," said my mother. "Most Japanese paper is made from mulberry bark. See how you don't know as much as you think you do, Hannah?"

The delivery man was pulling an enormous yellow box tied with string out of his van. He staggered off into the shop with it and my mother swept in after him, leaving me outside with the luggage. It crossed my mind that the Maekawas were taking delivery of my mother and me and that yellow box all at the same time. Mum had left one half of the sliding doors wide open behind her, and through it I could see long aluminum shelves of school writing books and notebooks and origami paper, a stand of letter sets and shiny-ribboned greeting cards, another of stickers and pencils, and a rack of brightly colored pencil cases. They looked fresh and orderly and tempting.

I love the smells of paper and ink. I'm one of those kids who loves all the things you find in a stationery store. I can spend hours looking at greeting cards, writing paper, felt pens and ballpoints. If I HAD to be part of my mother's excursion, I figured that living above a Japanese stationery shop would be some compensation. As the taxi slid away, I grasped a suitcase handle in each hand and headed for the door.

夂

Chapter Two

*A*fat, pumpkin-shaped lantern was the first thing I
noticed as I hauled my suitcases through the shop
doorway. Candlelit, it hung radiant orange in the dusty
darkness of one corner like a great beacon. A family crest,
three trees inside a stark black circle, was painted on its side.
Its light quivered across walls and floors, across the other
papery patterns and shapes around it, bending their sharp
edges and colors into hazy uncertainty.

That must be the Old Corner. The hot sticky scent of
melting wax drifted towards me, and traces of other, older
smells too: wet ink, moldy paste, and the sharpness of crushed
leaves.

The second thing I noticed was that my mother and the
delivery man were dancing around the shop. I had rarely seen
my mother dance, and never with a delivery man she'd only

just met. I was fascinated and I went a bit closer to investigate. It turned out that my mother had gotten a piece of the fake fur trim of her leopard-print coat hooked into one of the delivery man's gold buttons. He had her by the elbow and was pushing and pulling and trying to extricate himself. In the process they were performing a chaotic tango and making a lot of noise.

I tried to help but they wouldn't stand still, so I left them to it and went over to the counter. I thought there might be a bell I could ring to get attention.

The delivery man had put the yellow box on the counter before he tangled himself up with my mother. As I went towards it, it hissed. I took a step back. The box hissed again. Be calm, Hannah, I said to myself. It must be a cat. I tiptoed up and stuck my head around the box so I could see behind it. I nearly had a spasm! Peering out at me were a pair of wicked, black button eyes. They were attached to a skinny little granny. She was perched on a blue chair, and looked as old as winter. Her snowy hair was cut short and she was wearing a brown kimono and a cashmere shawl. Her feet in their white socks and wooden sandals barely touched the floor.

"*Sumimasen ga,*" I began. The granny turned her attention from the dancers at whom she'd been hissing and peered at me like an amused budgie. *Excuse yourself all you want*, she seemed to be saying. *It makes no difference to me.* Then she pointed behind her. So I shouted out, "*GOMENKUDASAI.*" Something breakable crashed to the floor. The door behind the counter shot open and a shaggy-banged man in glasses and a red apron erupted into the shop. He was carrying the two halves of a tea bowl. He stared at me, put the halves down and looked around. "Oooh!" he said. "Oooh! Oooh! Oooh!"

I agreed. What else could you say if you went away to have a quiet cuppa and while you were gone a woman with purple hair and a delivery man turned your shop into a dance hall?

He rushed over to them, brandishing a pair of scissors and shouting, "*CHOTTO MATTE. CHOTTO MATTE.*" They must have been getting tired, or perhaps the scissors frightened them, because they stood still and waited obediently so he could disentangle them. While they were rearranging themselves, he took a deep breath and straightened his apron.

"Mrs. Forrester," he said. "Welcome to Kanazawa." He turned to me. "It's nice to meet you, Hannah. I am Jun Maekawa."

The delivery man bowed and apologized about seventeen times, although I was sure the dancing wasn't his fault. As soon as he could get away he rushed out of the shop, probably in search of a strong drink. My mother has that effect on people. She handled the whole episode by pretending it hadn't happened, but she did remember to apologize for our earliness, and I was grateful for that.

Mr. Maekawa introduced us to Granny. "Granny lives with us most of the year but she spends summers at my elder sister's house in Nagano. It's cooler for her in the mountains. She always comes back to us at the end of autumn, because she likes to be in Kanazawa for the winter."

Granny bobbed her spiky white head in agreement. It was impossible to guess what she was thinking as she looked at us, but I had a feeling it wasn't too flattering.

Mr. Maekawa led us through the door behind the counter onto a little porch from which an impossibly narrow flight of stairs climbed at a sharp angle to the upper story. We took off our shoes and followed him. At the top of the stairs he turned right along a hallway, at the end of which were two rooms side by side. The one right at the end was the guest room where my mother would sleep that night. From tomorrow it would be my room. Just for this one night I'd be sharing the room next door with Miki. I was a bit nervous about sharing. I'm not one of those kids who likes bunking in with everybody else at sleepovers or school camps. I've always had my own room at home and I like privacy. I mean, what do you say to someone you've only just met? Especially someone a year older.

We dragged and gasped and thumped the luggage upstairs while Granny watched and nodded and hissed. I wondered if she was all right in the head. Then Mr. Maekawa said he'd make us some fresh tea. My mother, still obsessing about washing her clothes, went with him to find the laundry room, which he said was downstairs, near the bathroom, behind the kitchen. I was left alone in the guest room.

I went to look out the window. I always do that first if I'm staying somewhere different. I could see into the garden at the back of the house. A high stone wall enclosed a square moss floor of velvety green cut in half by a paved path. The path led to sliding doors that opened onto the lane beyond. A pine tree reached skywards, high above a stone lantern mossy with age. The pine looked a bit like an umbrella. Each of its branches were tied with straw rope to a bamboo pole sitting flush with the tree's trunk. I wondered why. I supposed it must be a windbreak. Or some kind of weird tree surgery.

There wasn't a bed in the room so I guessed we'd be sleeping Japanese-style. The floor was covered with *tatami* matting. Along the wall farthest from the door were an oil heater, a clothes cupboard and an alcove in which a scroll hung above a vase of pampas grass. In one corner a reading lamp stood on a low table. Near the door was a tiny dressing table with an elegant mirror.

I went and sat down on the *tatami* in front of it. The table was just level with my belly button and it had one tiny drawer. The mirror was long and narrow, its highest point well above my head. I ran my fingers along the birds and flowers engraved around its edges. Maybe a beautiful geisha had sat here once, pushing an ornamental hairpin of pink and white cherry blossoms into her hair. The best I'd be able to do was put on sunscreen. I wasn't even allowed to wear moisturizer.

It was odd to see my own face reflected in such a beautiful mirror. Joel, my horrible brother, says I have a squashed-up face. I tell him that's better than having a squashed-up brain like him. My face is square, with a short nose, so I guess maybe it does look a bit squashed up. My hair is thick and red-brown, just reaching my shoulders. I was the second shortest in my Year Seven class. Joel says I could double as a garden gnome. I told him he could start a butter factory just by bottling the grease on his repulsive face.

I leaned closer and peered into my round blue eyes. My green-eyed mother has a theory that foreigners' light eyes frighten elderly Japanese. This theory stems from the day she got on a bus in Kyoto and sat next to a granddad. The granddad got up and sat somewhere else. My mother insists the old man thought she had devil eyes. I suggested he probably thought that either he was sitting next to a dangerous lunatic or that he'd be asphyxiated by her Wild Wattle perfume. Wild Wattle is the world's pongiest. Liana loves it. I looked at my own face and wondered if it had frightened Granny Maekawa downstairs. I didn't think so. She hadn't looked frightened. She'd looked as if she'd just seen something hilarious.

My breath made a smudge patch on the mirror and I polished it with my sleeve. I wished I could rub the mirror like a magic lamp and have it tell me if I'd like staying in Kanazawa. Or maybe just how my dad was surviving all alone with germy Joel.

攵

Chapter Three

Kie Maekawa, my mother's friend, had been planning to drive to the station to pick us up, so she was really surprised to find us sitting in her living room when she arrived home. I was curious about Kie.

"What's she like?" I'd asked my mother on the plane.

Liana, digging away at her crème caramel, stopped and thought for a moment.

"She's like David Suzuki and Ita Buttrose rolled into one," she answered.

"So she's a Canadian-Japanese man with a small beard, great fashion sense and a lisp?"

My mother snorted and then haw-hawed, frightening the other passengers. "Don't be cute, Hannah." She hawed one more time and went back to her dessert.

I tried again. "What's her job?"

"She looks after the house and the family, and she does the accounts for the shop. Are you going to eat your crème caramel, Hannah?"

"Definitely," I said, moving it to the far side of my tray. "Does Mrs. Maekawa have any hobbies?"

My mother waved her spoon at me dismissively and shook her head.

"No, no. Kie has INTERESTS, not hobbies. She's PASSIONATE about environmental issues, and she belongs to a conservation group that works to protect Japan's wild animals. She goes to a macrobiotic cooking class. I think it's called 101 Ways to Use Brown Rice. But her BIG THING is recycling. You must be SURE to use the right bins, Hannah."

I soon found out my mother was right. Kie was a rabid recycler! She was president of the Kabuto Machi Ladies' Recycling Cooperative. In her kitchen she had five different colored bins – blue for paper, green for glass, pink for cans, purple for plastic, yellow for food scraps. It was as much as anyone's life was worth to put something in the wrong bin. Mr. Maekawa got into the most trouble. He couldn't seem to remember which bin was which, so he put things in the bins when no one was around. That way, when Kie found a banana skin among the glass, or a beer can in with the paper, he could say he didn't do it.

Kie pattered into the living room in stockinged feet, pulling off a pearl-grey coat and a blue scarf. Her hair was permed into curls that sat up around her face like fluffy meringue around a pie, so she looked really sweet and kind. Then I noticed her serious, steady eyes, and I knew that despite the sweetness and kindness there'd be no nonsense, which was why it was so hard to figure out her friendship with my mother!

They met in a Tokyo fish shop the first year we lived in Japan. My mother, for some mysterious reason, had decided to have a party. Neither her cooking nor her Japanese were very good in those days, but not being good at something has never stopped her trying to do it. She was sure she knew how to go shopping. All she had to do was say the name of the item she wanted, and add "*o kudasai*." Piece of cake! She stalked into the fish shop.

"*Kaba o kudasai.*"

"Eh?" said the young man behind the counter, looking very puzzled.

My mother decided he was a bit dim. "*Ka-ba o ku-da-sa-i,*" she said again, slowly and clearly.

The young man, alarmed, called the manager.

When the manager came out from the back of the shop, my mother tried again. She thought they might catch on if she spoke very loudly.

"*KABA O KUDASAI. KABA. KABA.*"

The manager dredged around in his head for his high school English. It took him a while to find it. "No big animals," he said. "Only fishes."

"*KABA,*" answered my mother. She wasn't the sort to exit

gracefully when things weren't going well. The manager, the assistant and the other customers were starting to panic when help walked in the door. Kie, in Tokyo visiting her parents, sized up the situation on the spot, guessing that even this odd foreigner didn't really want a hippopotamus.

"*Saba?*" said Kie.

"*SABA!! SABA!!*" yelled my mother.

She got her mackerel. The fish shop got rid of her. She and Kie had been great friends ever since.

Kie paused just inside the doorway, head tilted, smiling. "Such a lovely surprise that you're here already!"

My mother's nose popped out of her romance novel. She shrieked, leapt to her feet, pounded across the *tatami* and grabbed Kie's hands. "It's WONDERFUL to see you again! It's been FAR too long. SO kind of you to let Hannah stay."

Kie twinkled. "You haven't changed, Liana! Well, except for the hair. Welcome, Hannah. I'm so happy to meet you again. We've met before of course, but you'd have been too little to remember. Will we have some more tea?"

Miki came in from school about six-thirty. It had become very dark and a cold wind was buffeting the rain down the street. She had forgotten her umbrella and she was soaked and laughing, her clothes steaming in the sudden warmth of the house. The rain had plastered her hair flat to her head and the tail of her waist-length braid was dripping water behind her as she stood in the doorway. She had an oval face and a long nose and her grandmother's wicked black eyes. I liked

17

her right away. I hoped we'd be friends. I hoped she wouldn't think I was geeky or up myself like some of the kids at my school did.

As soon as she saw us sitting on the floor around the table she stopped laughing and put on a serious face. It made her look vague and innocent and a little bit sad.

She came just inside the room, sank to the floor with her legs tucked under her, and bowed. "I'm Mikiko. Nice to meet you."

I couldn't resist bowing back but I went a bit too low. I was sitting close to the table and the thwack of my head as it made contact was deafening. And it hurt. I sat gaping, knowing I was turning strawberry red. Visions of black eyes and broken noses ran across my brain. Miki started to laugh. Everyone did. Mrs. Maekawa giggled. My mother hawed. Mr. Maekawa, just coming in from the shop and looking sleepy and worried, cheered up instantly. Granny chortled the longest. In fact, she had chortling spasms all through dinner every time she caught my eye. It was very uncomfortable.

Aunt Yukiyo, Miki's father's younger sister, arrived to eat with us. The first thing that struck me was that she looked like a movie star. Her face was perfectly symmetrical, pale skin, jet-black hair. People who look like Snow White and not like a garden gnome are so lucky.

"I live next door, above my donut shop," she told me. "It's called the Honey House. Do you like donuts, Hannah?"

Did I like donuts?! Was Mount Fuji a volcano?!

I grinned and nodded. Aunt Yukiyo's smile lit up her whole face and danced around behind her eyes. A perfect movie star smile. "Good," she said.

I couldn't believe Miki was so late home from school. I knew that there was Saturday school in Japan, but surely only in the mornings. Detention crossed my mind, but it turned out she'd been at basketball club. Miki was crazy about basketball. She played almost every day after school and often on weekends. Despite looking like a puff of wind could blow her over, she was very fit and athletic. She was also a member of the school environment club. I wondered how she found time for it all. Later I realized she made time by doing as little schoolwork as possible.

We ate dinner sitting around the living room table on the floor. Popo, the family's sleepy charcoal cat, watched us from the top of the television set. Grandpa Honda, who owned the flower shop on the other side of the Mulberry Tree, came to dinner too. He was wearing a blue terrycloth hat so I guessed he must be like family. You have to know someone pretty well to go to dinner at their house in a blue terrycloth hat. He told me that his grandson, Hiro, lived with him but hadn't come to dinner because he was at cram school. I wondered why Hiro didn't live with his parents. I wondered what he studied at cram school.

Mrs. Maekawa cooked *jibu* – a Kanazawa specialty – in honor of our arrival. It's got this special ingredient called *sudarefu*. That's a wheat gluten paste unique to Kanazawa.

Sounds gruesome, but it isn't. It's delicious. As well as *fu*, *jibu* is made with duck meat, bamboo shoots, spinach, mushrooms and lily roots. They look like little white shells and taste like potatoes.

"The first Maeda lord at the castle ate *jibu*," said Aunt Yukiyo, when I'd gushed to her about how fabulous it was.

"The town was built up around it. But it burned down in –" Miki looked at her mother. "When, Mum?"

"Eighteen eighty-one." Mrs. Maekawa was definite. "Well over a hundred years ago. But the stone walls and the rear gate and armory are still standing in the town center."

"So there were battles and fighting and samurai killing each other with swords?"

"No. The Maedas were very clever. Kaga, that's the old name for the Kanazawa district, was Japan's wealthiest province. The Maedas wanted to keep it that way. Wars cost lots of money so they didn't want to have them. They developed trade and business and culture. They loved drama and music and gourmet foods like *jibu*. They were fond of the tea ceremony. One of them even made a handmade paper collection."

Grandpa Honda chimed in. He spoke slowly, like he was rolling his words around in his mouth, testing them before letting them out. "But the Maedas were a great warrior family and they were ready for war if it came. When you go to see the castle gate, Hannah *san*, you'll find that the roof is covered with white tiles. Very beautiful tiles made of lead. In an emergency, soldiers could melt them down for ammunition. And the windows in the castle walls were designed for dropping boulders."

His old eyes sparkled with excitement. I could picture the scene too. Soldiers everywhere – running, sweating above vats of molten lead, in position behind the windows, aware of the danger, of what a battle might cost them. It would be fun to see the walls of Kanazawa Castle, but I was glad the soldiers hadn't had to fight. Those beautiful white tiles were much better left on the roof.

"The Maedas ruled in a time in Japan's history called the Edo Period," said Aunt Yukiyo. "Edo is the old name for Tokyo. Japan's rulers built their castle there. It was a prosperous time in Japan, but difficult too. For two hundred and fifty years, contact with foreign lands was banned. Japanese were forbidden to leave Japan and no one who had left was allowed to come home."

"Did anyone leave?"

Aunt Yukiyo nodded. "I'm sure some did. But if they were caught, the punishments were severe."

Mrs. Maekawa stood up and went over to a chest of drawers near the door. She pulled out a map and came back to spread it on the table. "There's a lot to see in Kanazawa, Hannah. See, there's Kenrokuen, the garden of the Maeda lords. It has lakes and waterfalls and twelve thousand trees. And we have so many shrines and temples. Aunt Yukiyo has plans to show you the Ninja Temple. Here it is, in Teramachi."

A Ninja Temple sounded okay. I wasn't sure about the shrines and the gardens. What about shopping and video games? I scanned the map. Was there a Kanazawa Disneyland?

"That sounds nice, Mrs. Maekawa," I said aloud.

"Please call me Okaasan, Hannah. And call my husband Otōsan. You're family while you're with us,"

Okaasan, "Mum." Otōsan, "Dad." That was going to feel a bit weird.

Otōsan was polishing his glasses and pushing his bangs from side to side like a restless rabbit. Suddenly he stood up. "I think I'll go and unpack that yellow box and see if there are any treasures from Edo hidden in there," he said. "Perhaps Hannah and Miki would like to help me."

"Don't let Hannah be a BOTHER to you, Maekawa *san*," boomed my mother. "She has a TENDENCY to get OVEREXCITED."

Poor Mr. Maekawa looked alarmed to hear of my capacity for OVEREXCITEMENT. Or maybe it was the first time he'd heard anyone speak Japanese in capitals.

Chapter Four

There was a cold, papery whispering in the gloom outside the pool of light shed by the orange lantern. It was only the night breeze and the murmur of rain slipping in under the door, teasing paper edges, but it felt eerie. Mr. Maekawa, that is, Otōsan, bustled over to a lamp and switched it on. Light fell onto the back wall of the Old Corner, revealing a huge centipede with a red tongue hanging from its blue-eyebrowed, black and yellow face. I jumped, then pretended I hadn't.

Miki, putting down a beanbag doorstop to block the wind, laughed. "It's only a kite."

The Old Corner was extraordinary. Paper origami cranes in pink and purple flew from the ceiling and green frogs swam on a sheet of aqua silk along one wall. Miki and her father showed me red and purple parasols, paper dolls in kimonos, and a yellow tiger. And masks. An old woman with her face wrapped in a blue and white spotted kerchief and a red leering man with crossed eyes hung among paper balloons and ornate fans painted with mountains and willow trees. Books packed tightly on shelves seemed to carry imprints of long ago fingers. And paper lanterns hung everywhere, bright red ones for *sake* shops, others painted with flowers and faces, and old ones with green leaf patterns and square wooden handles.

"Paper is the source of history and wisdom," said Otōsan, gazing at his hoard like a proud father. "Without it, nothing would ever have been written down."

Miki straightened a warrior mask. "Dad says paper's like a person," she said. "Tough and long-lasting, but easily hurt if it's not treated well. What do you like best, Hannah?"

I gazed around at all the lovely shapes and colors. "I like everything!"

They both laughed.

"So do I, Hannah," said Otōsan. "That's why I don't sell much from the Old Corner. I can't bear to part with my treasures."

I understood. I would have loved them too if they were mine.

"Professor Kato sent this," explained Otōsan, as Miki cut the strings from the yellow box. "The professor's a paper collector like me. He and his wife have lived in the same home for fifty years, since they married. It's close to that Ninja Temple you're going to visit. Kato's ancestors built the house two hundred years ago, but it's now falling down. The government wants to demolish it and put a new road through."

Miki rolled the string into a ball and slipped it in her pocket. "That must be so sad for the Katos."

"It is and it isn't," answered Otōsan. "The Katos can't maintain the old place any longer, and the government is building them a modern house out near the university. The professor phoned me a few days ago to tell me he was clearing out his study and was sending me some things I might find interesting. Let's see if he's right."

Miki's dad reached into the box with church-like reverence and pulled out six or seven old books made of thin greenish-yellow paper, the calligraphy on the covers faded and spidery. He set them carefully aside. I felt a wild power surge of excitement as each book was revealed. Maybe my mother was right and I did have a tendency to HYSTERIA.

Next was a shiny, pinkish-brown fan. Otōsan was so elated, his glasses fogged up. "A war fan. The first I've ever had. Exquisite. See how the frame is made of metal? A samurai could use it to parry sword blows in battle."

He started leaping around, cutting through the air with the fan. I ducked for cover but Miki ignored him and went on rifling through the box. She pulled out paper cutouts that looked like squares of lace, and a book made up of sheets of decorated paper, like carpet samples. I thought it was really pretty.

"Ahhh," breathed Miki's father, landing daintily and taking it from her. "A *chiyogami* collection. Wonderful."

Miki rolled her eyes. "Decorated paper," she explained to me. "Dad's the one who gets OVEREXCITED."

She opened the lid of a tattered rectangular box. It was the size of a shoebox, brown faded to buff and yellow-edged, as if it might have once gotten wet. I watched a silvery dust rise from it like incense. Smelled an old fishy whiff.

Miki unpacked its contents with careful fingers. "Old toys," she said, lifting out a stick with strips of paper hanging off it. "Look, a *hata genpei*."

Otōsan explained. "Like a whirligig. It blows around in the wind. Very popular in the old days."

A carved wooden rowboat with miniature oars sat easily on Miki's curved palm. Otōsan was examining some beautiful black and white shells as if they were precious stones. "A game of *Go*," he said. "Like checkers."

"With shells?" I'd never heard you could play checkers with shells.

Miki had found a set of cards wrapped in thin blue paper. "Look, Dad. Flower cards."

I peered over her shoulder, wondering what flower cards could be. Something for collecting? Like baseball cards?

"It's a traditional game, Hannah," said Miki. "There are forty-eight cards, four for each month, twelve for each season. You can still buy sets in department stores but these are really old."

As she flicked through the cards I saw they were all pictures of flowers or trees. Cherry blossoms, chrysanthemums, pine trees, irises and lots of others I couldn't identify. A few cards had pictures of animals with the trees and flowers. A deer, a frog, a wild boar.

"Can I borrow them, Dad? I'll show Hannah how to play."

"Why don't we give them to Hannah as a souvenir?" Otōsan was beaming. "A truly traditional Japanese gift for you, Hannah."

I took the cards, liking the silky feel of the blue paper. They sat snug in my palm, like the touch of a small, familiar hand. "Thank you," I said. "They're lovely."

"What's this?" There were a few other odds and ends in the box, buttons and pins and material scraps, but Miki was scraping at something with her nails. It seemed to be stuck to one wall of the box. She pulled out a pale, creased square of paper covered in the same spidery calligraphy as the books. She looked closely at it, half puzzled, half amused.

"It's old Japanese," she said. "I can't read all the *kanji*."

Otōsan looked over her shoulder. "Some of those *kanji* aren't used any more, but I recognize most of them. Let's see if I can decipher it." He shook back his bangs, pushed his glasses further up his nose and began to read haltingly.

If you, finder, choose to help the ocean boy,
Wait for the first snowfall.
The flute player at the temple of secrets
has the fox light.
At the hour of the bull bring the light to the shrine
Where women go to poison the hearts of their rivals.
After the bean throwing
Take the talisman you receive

To the place where the old mountain god
waits in the forest.
With the gift and your winter words from
the house of cards
Go at sunrise to wake the dragon that
sleeps in the lord's garden.
But beware the one
Who does not want the boy to go.
And remember always:
Blue for safety, yellow is warning, red means danger.

The words hovered for a moment like butterflies in the shop's yellow silence. Behind us, beyond the pool of light that spilled from the lamp, the old papery things whispered. Above them the orange lantern swayed gently.

When Miki spoke, her voice was prickly with excitement. "What does it mean, Dad? Who is the ocean boy?"

Her dad went over and switched on the fluorescent light. Its harshness scattered the lantern and lamp lights and broke the papery spell, but a tingling unease edged its way on down my spine.

"The ocean boy? It's an odd phrase, but this is old writing. He was probably one of the professor's ancestors. It may have been the child who owned the toys. But if he needed help, it's too late now. He's been gone a long time."

He put the lid back on the toy box. "You girls better go to

bed or I'll be in trouble with Okaasan. I hope you enjoy the cards, Hannah. Goodnight."

"*Oyasuminasai*," answered Miki as she slid open the door to the stairs.

"*Oyasuminasai*," I echoed, and closed it behind me.

It was cold on the stairs. I shivered, and a sudden breeze pulled the cards from my hands. They fountained into the air, then dropped down around us like small, rectangular leaves.

"That's odd," said Miki. "There's never any wind in here when the doors are closed." She looked around curiously to see where the breeze might have come from.

I picked up two cards that had landed near my feet. They felt solid, like cardboard, and a bit sticky.

It took us ages to find them all because Popo the cat came to play and kept sitting on them.

Miki's bedroom was toasty warm and smelled like kerosene. Okaasan had been in and turned on the oil heater. I put the cards with the rest of my things. Miki showed me the cupboard where the futons, pillows and blankets were stored during the day, and I helped her set up a bed for each of us on the *tatami*. I wasn't looking forward to sleeping on the floor. A futon doesn't have inner springs and I'm keen on comfort.

Before sliding in under the blankets I switched off the light and went over to the window. Rain was making puddles in the garden and dripping from the old pine's branches. A square-headed man in a long coat strode down the lane under a dark umbrella, talking into a mobile phone. The raindrops on his coat shimmered like sequins in the light of the streetlamps.

"What are you looking at?" Miki had come back from cleaning her teeth and was standing beside me.

I didn't want her to think I was nosy. "The garden," I said quickly. "Why are the trees tied up?"

"That's *yukitsuri*. We rope the trees because of the snow. Here on the Japan Sea coast our snow is wet, so it's very heavy. If the trees aren't roped, their branches break under its weight."

"Snow?"

I hadn't thought of snow. Not much snow falls in Tokyo, but I had a vague memory of seeing it once when I was little. Zigzags of excitement ran around the back of my skull. Snow. Castles. Exotic temples. Yellow boxes. Japan was getting more and more interesting.

Popo leapt onto the windowsill and crouched there staring out into the night. Thunder rolled and rumbled over the eastern mountains.

"*Buri okoshi*," said Miki dreamily.

"What's *buri okoshi*?"

"*Buri* are yellowtail, Kanazawa's favorite fish. We say that winter thunder wakes them up. They come closer to the surface of the Japan Sea in the cold weather, so in the winter it's easier to catch them."

I thought of what the sea would be like tonight. Dark and deep and bitter, white caps tossing. Thunder crackled again, booming across the sky, and a sharp flash of yellow lightning split the darkness. I had my hand on Popo's thick fur, felt him shudder. A sudden vicious gust of wind hurled a flurry of wet leaves against the windowpane. Suddenly I felt a long way from home.

"Hey, there's Hiro."

Miki tapped her knuckles on the glass, but the boy in the lane either didn't hear or chose not to. He looked windblown, and very wet, walking slowly, head bent against the downpour, feet kicking at puddles. Both hands were shoved deep in his coat pockets and a schoolbag bumped on his shoulder. This must be Hiro Honda, the boy from the shop next door.

"Why does he look so miserable?"

Miki sighed. "He's gotten like that in the last year, since his dad disappeared. Mr. Honda went south to Yonaguni Island for his work. He was supposed to be gone just one month, but he never came back."

"Really?"

Of course I wanted to ask more questions, but like I said, I didn't want her to think I was nosy. It could wait. She switched off the heater and we slid into the warmth of our futons.

Mine was comfortable except for the pillow. "Miki, there's something wrong with my pillow."

"What sort of something?"

"It's making a scritching noise. Like mice."

"Wheat husks," said Miki.

31

"Pardon?"

"The pillow's full of wheat husks. To make you clever."

"I'm already clever."

"Maybe you'll get cleverer. It's never worked for me." She giggled, then yawned. "Sleep well, Hannah."

That first night in Kanazawa, snug above the Mulberry Tree with rain falling all around, I dreamt of falling paper. Little colored origami animals, strands of shiny paper ribbon in red and gold, letters and paper lanterns and pages from a diary. And the wind rose and rose, whirling them all in circles, draining the colors from them until they had all been torn to shreds of white and began to fall like snow.

攵

Chapter Five

My mother left for Tokyo the next morning, but not
before she'd woken the household at dawn by falling
down the stairs. I had barely opened my eyes, was lying
looking out through the window at a pearly sky touched with
rose. The rain had stopped. I drifted, snuggled back into the
warmth of my futon. Then, BOOM. CRASH. On the other
side of the room Miki exploded out of her blanket mound like
a distressed mole in spotty pajamas.

Mum had landed on the bottom step like a misguided
ballet dancer, one leg folded under her and both arms in the
air. She'd lost her slippers on the way down. But she was still
talking.

"… SUCH a gust of wind. My hand slid RIGHT OFF
the rail. My slippers flew RIGHT OUT from under me. I
can't think HOW it happened."

I couldn't either. Too much moisturizer on her hands?

"Are you okay, Mum?"

"I think so, darling. I may have wrenched my ankle."

Miki and I helped her into the kitchen and Okaasan put the kettle on for tea. Mum said she'd like Aussie tea with sugar so I went upstairs to her room to find her emergency teabag supply. I looked closely at the stairs, ran my hand over the banister as I climbed. Old wood. Nothing tricky here. Or was there? A frosty little breeze ruffled my hair and I remembered last night and the flight of the flower cards.

By ten, Mum's foot had stopped hurting and she was waiting for a taxi at the shop entrance. We all waited with her: Otōsan, Okaasan, Miki, me and Granny, who someone had put outside in the sun. Aunt Yukiyo came out of her shop wearing a black and yellow striped apron with bees embroidered on the pockets. In daylight she looked more like a movie star than ever. Grandpa Honda bowed and waved from his flower shop. In her stylish grey suit Mum looked amazing, despite the hair. We gave each other a big hug.

"I'll be back to see you soon, sweetheart. Work hard on your *kanji* and make sure those correspondence lessons get done. Don't give Kie any trouble. And enjoy yourself." Then she zoomed off to Komatsu Airport, leaving me alone in Kanazawa.

Scents of cinnamon and chocolate and warm sugar drifted into the sunny air from the Honey House. Aunt Yukiyo must have noticed me drooling. Or maybe she thought I was upset because my mother had gone. I was a bit, but I didn't intend to show it. Anyhow, she invited Miki and me in for a drink and a donut.

The Honey House had pale-green walls on which painted bees skimmed and dived in a garden of giant flowers. The donuts were set out under the counter in glass cases, with their names printed below them in *katakana*. Caramel Mystery. Banana Dream. Jimmy Jammy. I chose a Raspberry Nightmare. Hot raspberries and chocolate syrup inside and sugar on top. Hannah in heaven. Miki had a Cherry Crunchy. We both had hot tea.

"Does Aunt Yukiyo have children?"

We were sitting at a forest-green table near the window. Miki shook her head and looked knowledgeable. "Aunt Yukiyo never married. That was because of Mr. KimiShimi."

"Mr. Who?"

"It's not his real name. At least it's not all of his name. His first name was Kimi something and his surname was Shimi something. My mother always calls him KimiShimi. We all do. He broke Aunt Yukiyo's heart and she left Kanazawa. She went to live in Aomori Prefecture to forget KimiShimi."

"That's so romantic. What did he do to break her heart? And where's Aomori?"

"Aomori is Honshu's most northern prefecture. Aunt Yukiyo lived for ten years on the Shimokita Peninsula, right at its northern end. The peninsula's a strange kind of place. Aunt Yukiyo told me there are gorges and waterfalls and forests, and in some places sulfur oozes from the ground. And there's a mountain where old, blind soothsayers speak with the dead. And the weather's very wild." Miki's black eyes lit up at the thought of such wildness and mystery.

"What did your aunt do there?"

"She opened a restaurant specializing in Kanazawa cuisine. She's a bit mysterious herself so I think living there suited her. I don't know if she forgot KimiShimi, because no one will give me any information. They won't tell me how he broke her heart either. Maybe she's never said."

I glanced over at Aunt Yukiyo. She was behind the counter, wiping down round, orange trays with a yellow cloth. She looked beautiful, but not mysterious or brokenhearted.

"Why did she come back? And what happened to KimiShimi?"

"She said Kanazawa called her, that the time was right. She came back two years ago and opened the Honey House. I never heard what happened to KimiShimi. I don't think anyone's seen him." Miki put her tea cup down. "Should we go for a walk so you get to know the neighborhood a bit?"

Okaasan came with us. The air was clean and cutting after the rain of the day before. Water lay in pools and puddles on the street so we had to step around them. Masses of flowers were clustered under the red awning of Grandpa Honda's shop but no one was in sight, so I was surprised when Okaasan called out.

"Hiro *chan*. Come and meet our friend Hannah."

A giant black chrysanthemum rose up from among the tulips and daisies, disturbing two ginger kittens who'd been sleeping on an upturned bucket. The chrysanthemum revealed itself to be a spiky, black head above a determined face. Hiro Honda, dry. He was a bit taller than me, half a head shorter that Miki, and made me think of a mushroom with attitude. I wondered why he'd been lurking in the flowers. Then I saw the watering can in his hand.

"It's nice to meet you," said Hiro, bowing.

I did a quick check to make sure no hard furniture was in range and bowed back.

"Come for a walk with us, Hiro," suggested Miki. "You can practice your English with Hannah. Hiro learns English at cram school."

"*E?! Samui yo*," said Hiro quickly. Now he looked like a mushroom determined not to speak English.

Miki giggled. "Too cold for you to go walking just now, Hiro? Okay, we'll leave you alone. See you in the morning."

We sauntered on towards the river. There are two rivers in Kanazawa, the masculine Sai and the feminine Asano. The Japanese often say things are masculine or feminine. Black pine trees are masculine, red pines are feminine. Mulberry paper is masculine, but paper from the mitsumata tree is feminine. I think it's weird, but my mother told me NEVER TO SAY THAT TO A JAPANESE PERSON. So I didn't mention it when Okaasan told me about the rivers, even though I would have liked to ask for an explanation.

The Mulberry Tree was in an old part of town called Kabuto Machi, where thin streets and impossible flights of stairs twist and turn down to the Asano River. Two-storied wooden shops and restaurants huddled together, tiled roofs shining wet in the winter sun. Tea-colored and chocolate brown, their wooden walls soaked up the sunshine like grateful granddads warming their backs. Black and white *noren* curtains hung from the eaves, announcing the proprietor's family name and what each shop sold – tea, soy sauce, candy, *fu*, dolls, traditional cakes, incense.

"It's like traveling backwards in time." I said.

Okaasan smiled at me, her serious eyes warm. "You're quite right, Hannah," she said. "Kanazawa's old stories lie just below its present – a bit like shadows under shallow water. It's as if the past is still alive all around. When I came from Tokyo to marry Miki's father, I noticed it immediately. Tokyo is busy, crowded and polluted, high rise and high tech. Old Japan is still there, but it's hard to find."

I looked ahead at the aged shops, their upper stories overhanging the street.

"Do you mean," I asked, "that people from the past are still here? Like … ghosts?"

"I do." Okaasan answered without hesitation. I looked at her to see if she was joking. She didn't seem to be.

"I don't mean ghosts that float around and wail and rattle

things, Hannah," she went on. "I don't see or hear them …
but I feel their presence. It's as if their shadows take shape out
of the old places preserved in the city: the temples and shrines
and samurai houses. I feel them strongest deep in winter,
when the year is oldest. Eastern winters are mild and sunny,
but in Kanazawa winters are dark and cold and snowy. We say
western Japan lies in the east's shadow. Perhaps in our winter
dark, the screens between past and present thin and weaken,
and ghosts slip more easily between the two."

She smiled at me, her eyes trance-like. Pure nuttiness, I
thought. Maybe now I could see the Liana connection!

"How do you know the ghosts are there?" I asked.

"You can feel them. You might walk down a street in a
sleety wind, or shelter from the snow under temple eaves, and
you feel someone beside you, someone who belonged in that
place hundreds of years ago."

Now she was giving me the shivers. I didn't want to
feel any ghosts and I certainly didn't want them feeling me.
Miki looked at my face and started to giggle. "Hoooo," she
moaned. "Beware, Hannah Forrester. The winter spirits are
watching."

I laughed too. So did Okaasan.

"I'm sorry, Hannah," she said, "I didn't mean to alarm
you. It's just that the presence of the old spirits is so real for
me and it's one of the things I love about the city. And by the
way, Mikiko has no reason to make fun. She's a believer in
ghosts herself."

"Well, I half believe," said Miki. "But that's mainly because of Dad."

"Ah, your father," said Okaasan, shaking her curly head. "Now, he dances to a different tune altogether!"

I wondered what she meant. I supposed I'd find out soon enough. Otōsan did seem a bit unusual.

"When do you think it will start to snow?" I asked.

Okaasan looked up at pale-grey sky patched with wintry blue. Heavy clouds were building dark on the horizon, closing in over the city. An icy wind was rising. Its chill reminded me of the breeze on the stairs.

"December was unusually warm and the snow is late. But tonight or tomorrow it will come. It always snows soon after the *buri okoshi*."

The Asano River ran silvery chill. Willows grew along its banks, and cherry trees stripped bare. A great brown kite, wings spread wide, circled high above us. Ducks swam in and out of the reed clumps. I could see curved bridges upstream and downstream, pedestrians and traffic moving to-and-fro across them. I thought I spotted the mobile phone man, the one who'd been in the lane the night before, striding across the upstream bridge. He had the same squarish head. In daylight I could see his phone was red.

"Hannah will have to get some new boots," said Miki as we were walking back to the Mulberry Tree.

"Will I? Why?" I looked down protectively at my shiny new lace-ups. They'd cost a fortune, but I'd persuaded my mother I'd use them A LOT because they were fleecy lined. They made me feel fabulous. And tall.

"Kanazawa boots for Kanazawa," said Miki, looking wise.

"Huh?"

"Your boots are gorgeous, Hannah, but when it starts to snow you'll need waterproofs. Those will get too damp and the soles won't hold you on the ice. Japan Sea coast snow is wet. Remember how I told you the tree branches can't take its weight? You should be able to buy some snow boots cheap. I think I saw some at a shoe store in the main street, on special for 2000 *yen*. Mum could show you while I'm at school."

"Or," said Okaasan, "I could lend you a pair of mine. Best to save 2000 *yen* for something you really want to spend it on. Don't you think so, Hannah?"

I certainly did think so. What a sensible Okaasan.

夂

Chapter Six

*O*kaasan gave me some floral terrycloth slippers to wear in the house. Brand new scuffs with no heels. I had problems keeping them on but I liked the sound of them flapping and slapping.

Wearing shoes in a Japanese home is something you just DON'T DO. It's like picking your nose in public in Australia. No one will speak to you if you do it, and everybody thinks you're dirty and badly brought up. The Japanese say the ground is unclean. Unclean things don't belong inside a house. Shoes touch the ground so they don't belong in a house. Simple.

But I wasn't used to thinking much about shoes, and I made a few mistakes. The second day, I walked on the *tatami* in my slippers. Granny spotted me and from that instant appointed herself captain of the shoe police. Any time I was close to making a shoe boo-boo, Granny would materialize like a tiny bent conjuring trick. I don't know how she did it. She didn't talk much but she liked her shoe lecture. I heard it so many times I soon knew it by heart.

"At the house door, outdoor shoes off, house slippers on. Entrance to a *tatami* room, house slippers off, socks or bare feet only. Toilet, special case. House slippers off, toilet slippers on, go to the toilet, toilet slippers off, house slippers back on."

It was more complicated than a quadruple bypass. The day I wore my regular slippers into the toilet nobody saw me, but I suffered terrible guilt for hours.

The shoe boxes inside the garden entrance helped me remember. Shoe boxes look like shelves of pigeonholes but they're full of shoes instead of papers. The Maekawas put good shoes in the boxes and left their everyday shoes in a line on the floor of the entrance room. Whenever I saw the boxes and the shoe lineup I'd remember to take mine off.

On Monday morning I stood beside the shoe boxes and watched Miki jam on her school sneakers without undoing the laces. Mum had arranged for me to go to school every Wednesday and Friday because Miki's class had a double Japanese lesson both days. So I couldn't go with her until Wednesday, and I felt mournful and left out. Miki was wearing her school uniform, a navy dress with a crimson sailor collar and a navy sweater. Her legs were bare except for thick white ankle socks.

"Won't you be cold without tights?"

"No, I'm okay."

Even when the temperature's below zero, Japanese junior high girls won't wear tights or stockings to school. It's not cool. I wore mine. I've never been cool, and I'm probably never going to be, and I didn't like having cold legs.

Miki shrugged into her duffle coat. "I'll come home early today, Hannah," she said. "I won't be going to the club. Aunt Yukiyo's taking us to the Winter Street Festival in Temple Town and to the Ninja Temple. Hiro's coming too."

"I know. Okaasan told me. I'm totally excited." Although I would have preferred to go without gloomy Hiro Honda.

In the meantime, I had the day to fill. Back in my room I wandered around for a bit, tidying my stuff and looking out the window. Yesterday's sun had vanished and the day was cold and windless. The flower cards were on my table and I picked them up and unwrapped the blue paper. I sorted through them and picked out the ones I liked best. The deer with red and yellow maple leaves, I decided, and a green-grey hillside under a full moon.

The purple of the irises conjured up a vision of my mother's hair, spurring me on to find the *kanji* practice book she'd bought me. I flipped through its pages and found I already knew some of the *kanji*. I knew "day" and "month," because one of us wrote the date on the blackboard at the start of every Japanese lesson in Year Five. I knew *Nihongo*, the word for "Japanese." Japanese teachers always make you write *Nihongo* in color on the title page of your Japanese book. It's made up of three *kanji*: *ni*, "sun", which is the same as "day";

hon is "book", but also means "origin"; *go* means "language."

We'd learned the days of the week, and numbers one through ten, in Year Six. I knew "big" and "small", and "ear", "mouth", "eye", and "hand." *Mae*, "in front of", and *kawa*, "river", Maekawa. And *hana*, "flower." I knew *hana* because its sound is close to Hannah. My teacher had shown me how to write it so I could use it as my Japanese name, even though in appearance and personality I'm not very flowery.

I counted them up. I already knew thirty. That left just nine hundred and seventy to go. Yeah right, Mum. I listened to the satisfying sound of myself sighing tragically and opened the book at the "nature" section. I'd start with "sky", "wind", "cloud", "sea" and "mountain." At least those were real things I'd seen or felt, and I could picture them in my head.

"Snow is forecast for this afternoon, Hannah," said Okaasan, as she put a steaming bowl of noodles in front of me at lunchtime. We were eating with Granny in the kitchen. Otōsan had already eaten and was back in the shop.

"The forecasters are usually right," Okaasan continued after a mouthful of noodles. "Why don't you work down here and keep me company, and we'll watch it begin together."

The gas heater was burning and the room was cozy and yellow-warm. After we'd washed up I started a math correspondence lesson. Okaasan tuned in to some classical music on the radio and began work on the shop's account books. Granny sat by the window, looking out into the garden and humming softly along with the radio. I kept an eye on the window too. The old pine's branches rose stark black against its white ropes, needles gleaming emerald in the witch-light climbing across the sky.

It began mid-afternoon. Thunder rolled and rolled again. I thought of the yellowfish surfacing in salty waters, icy waves raging and crashing around them. Wind swept the first snow in hard, spitting and biting at the window panes. Then the wind dropped and snow was tumbling soft from the sky, gentle as flower petals. I wanted to be outside, wanted to see what snow felt like. Okaasan was reluctant to let me go at first, but she relented when I promised to dress warmly and come inside the minute I felt cold. She wrapped me up in layers of socks and gloves and scarves and sweaters until I looked like a neurotic sumo wrestler, and she lent me a pair of snow boots. Then I waddled outside into the garden, making the first footprints on fresh snow. It felt like the beginning of an adventure.

夂

Chapter Seven

At five o'clock, Hiro was waiting for us in front of the flower shop, spiky and determined in jeans and boots. One hand was in the pocket of his grey parka, the other clutched a gigantic umbrella of red and yellow tartan. When he saw us he opened it and marched silently on to the snow-scattered road, a serious soldier rejoining the regiment. I wondered sourly if he ever spoke. Or smiled.

The snow was a mobile curtain of white beads. We all had umbrellas but some of the beads snuck in under them. They got caught in the ends of Miki's black hair and on the legs of Hiro's jeans, and settled along the sleeves of Aunt Yukiyo's blue coat. I'd always wanted a curtain of glass beads to hang in front of my bedroom door, strings of beads in red and blue and green that would click whenever the wind blew. My mother said UNDER NO CIRCUMSTANCES because they're CHEAP and NASTY. Maybe I could persuade her that white had more class.

We walked up from Kabuto Machi and took a short cut through Omicho Market. Fluorescent lights illuminated fruit and vegetable stalls stacked with apples from Aomori, potatoes from Hokkaido, bamboo shoots from Kyushu, bananas from the Philippines, water chestnuts, lotus roots and bunches of tiny yellow mushrooms. I almost fell into a plastic bucket of seaweed roots because I was staring at the crabs. Pink, red, white, hairy, big, small, huge mounds of them. And trays of miniature grey octopus with wistful eyes. Miki told me their insides look like boiled rice so I wasn't sure if I'd like to eat them. We passed frozen salmon and spotty sea cucumbers, and Aunt Yukiyo went to a lot of trouble to find a blowfish to show me. I was interested in blowfish – *fugu* in Japanese. You can eat them, but they carry lethal poison in their ovaries and if they're not properly prepared they can kill you. Once I saw a reporter eat one on a TV show called "Special Correspondent." I can still remember how strangely disappointed I was when he was alive at the end of the program.

By the time we reached the bus stop, so much snow had piled up on my umbrella that it was almost too heavy to hold. Miki showed me the Kanazawa umbrella shake. She stood still under her umbrella, put both hands on the handle and shook it hard. The snow tumbled off and she stayed dry.

"See," said Miki, "how wet the snow is?"

Okay. Okay. I got the point. The snow was wet!

I understood now why she'd said I'd need waterproof boots. Underfoot was very sloshy. This was partly caused by water fountaining out of little silver holes in the pavement. Lines of holes ran down the middle of the roads too. The spouting water helped melt the snow so pedestrians didn't slip and hurt themselves and cars didn't skid.

It was my first time in a Japanese bus. Maybe I had been in one before, when I was little and lived in Tokyo, but I didn't remember. It was rush hour and the bus was packed, but I didn't mind because all the body heat kept me warm. The bus rules were different from Australia's. We got in the back door and left by the front. We paid when we got off instead of when we got on. There was an illuminated board above the driver's head that told you how much you had to pay. And the driver was wearing a cap and gloves. Not woolen gloves to keep warm, but white cotton gloves. He looked as if he should be going to a ball.

It was getting dark. The bus was stopping and starting in traffic, so I got a good look at central Kanazawa. Brightly lit buildings and department stores, and neon signs in red, orange and green colored the snowy dusk. Long pink and red placards advertised Valentine's Day. Along the footpaths, tiny gold lights shone from the spindly, naked branches of thin trees, like delicate hands in black jeweled gloves. Orange light cones mimicked the shapes of the roped pine trees.

We stopped at a red light and Aunt Yukiyo pointed left up

a wide avenue. "The castle gate's up that way." She peered out the window. "I hope this traffic eases up. I don't want to keep Mr. Sawaguchi waiting."

People hurried by under a sea of umbrellas, tramping on the snow in high rubber boots. Some girls wore miniskirts even though it was such cold weather. Most of the men were in black suits or long grey coats. Snow was piling up on car roofs and walls and tree branches.

"Mr. Sawaguchi," explained Miki, "is a friend of Aunt's. He works at the temple. Look, that's the Sai River."

We were crossing a curved bridge. I looked down at gunmetal-grey water and riverbanks white with snow.

We left the bus a minute later, and the cold wrapped itself around us as we turned left towards Temple Town, following the muffled beating of *taiko* drums.

The street of the Ninja Temple was closed to vehicles for the evening because of the festival, and stalls were set up outside temples, tea houses and craft shops. Wonderful smells wafted past. Hot noodles, fish cakes, bean jam buns, soy sauce, and ice cream. The snowy darkness was lit with fires and lanterns. We threaded our way through the crowd. Hiro tangled himself up with twin toddlers carrying silver balloons, which made him cross. Their mother had a little dog tucked inside her coat and she let Miki and me pat him. Some of the ladies were dressed in kimonos with fur stoles around their shoulders. We made our way through them all towards the Ninja Temple. Our appointment was for six.

In the temple courtyard it was quieter than silence. We passed under a great tree and the temple came out of the gloom towards us, its pointed roof white against black sky. Mr. Sawaguchi was waiting in the entrance hall, grasping an enormous flashlight. He looked at us gravely with his long, damp face. His name suited him perfectly. Mr. "Entrance to the Marsh." Aunt Yukiyo made introductions and we bowed. I was beginning to feel more comfortable bowing, less like an elephant trying to do tricks.

In other ways I wasn't comfortable at all. The floor crackled with frost and my feet snap-froze to blocks of ice as soon as we took off our shoes. I was unsettled by the cold and the dim lighting, and by Mr. Sawaguchi's sad moistness. Suddenly I wished my mother was beside me, booming and stumbling and chasing the gremlins away.

Mr. Sawaguchi asked us in his wet voice to sit on a red carpet beside the Buddhist altar. He would tell us the temple's history before showing us the rooms. Oh good, a lecture! I looked around at ornate hangings and golden bells and the sumptuous altar where the Maeda lords came to pray. Guards carrying swords weren't allowed to approach this holy place, Mr. Sawaguchi told us. The lord didn't pray in front of the altar either, but in a hidden room above, sitting on the dark side of a blind that worked like a magic mirror. I glanced up. Were eyes watching us from that dark corner? Had I seen a flicker of movement?

The temple was a fortress as well as a place of prayer,

but it wasn't called Ninja because *ninja* used it. That was disappointing to hear. It was exactly the sort of place where you could imagine masked spies creeping around in black clothes, peering and listening and poisoning enemies. It was called the Ninja Temple because it had so many places to hide. *Ninjutsu* is the art of concealment.

Mr. Sawaguchi droned on. In the Edo Period, one thousand samurai could be garrisoned here, ready to defend their lord and his territory. At the highest point of the temple roof, guards watched from the lookout in all weathers. They could see the castle to the east, the mountains and the main highway to the southwest, and the Sea of Japan to the northwest. If an enemy was moving on the roads or by sea, the samurai at the Ninja Temple would know.

I wanted to move, but the history lesson dragged on. A chill was creeping along my bones and I felt weird. When we finally got up for the tour, my legs didn't want to carry me. Mr. Sawaguchi sagged along in front, showing us deep pits under the floor, invisible in the gloom. An enemy could fall three meters into a pit where a samurai waited in the dark to kill. Under a moveable floorboard, an escape stair to the outside of the building ran down into blackness. A trick door concealed a cupboard-sized hiding place. One room had five secret exits, but I couldn't see any of them until Mr. Sawaguchi showed us where they were. We saw stairs with the vertical part made of translucent paper, so a watcher behind the stairs could see whose legs were going up and down.

My brain knew it was fascinating, but all the time a gnawing sense of uneasiness was growing inside me. It was so dark. I felt so lonely. I wanted desperately to tell Mr. Sawaguchi to be quiet. Talking seemed too dangerous. I glanced at the others. Aunt smiled at me. Miki was absorbed. Hiro's face was blank.

Colder and colder. We'd reached the center of the temple, and a round well, built of stone from Mount Tomuro.

"The well falls to a depth of twenty-five meters," murmured Mr. Sawaguchi. "The temple was built around it."

As we stood looking down into the well's dimness, I began to feel light-headed. Mr. Sawaguchi was telling us the legend of a secret tunnel that ran underground to the banks of the Sai River. The ruling lord would use it for secret business, lowering himself into the well on a rope until he reached the tunnel mouth. Once in the tunnel he could find his way to a hidden exit on the Sai River's bank, from which a secret road led to the castle.

The guide's wet voice whispered down the well. "Every carpenter who helped to build the tunnel was killed. To keep the secret safe."

Cold hands gripped at my stomach and my skin went hot. I was falling, past Aunt Yukiyo's concerned face and Hiro's surprised one. I could feel my right hand scraping at damp stones. The left one was burning like fire and slipping, slipping. I couldn't hold on. I couldn't. I was going to fall.

Miki grabbed my arm. "Hannah, are you okay?"

I nodded, pulled myself upright. I was shivering as I wiped away the beginning of tears. "I'm fine," I muttered. "Just so cold."

I thought for a minute I was going to be sick. Why was I feeling so weird and scared? I love creepy stories and I'm not easily frightened. But the air of that well was empty and cold and bleak. I took a deep breath and told myself not to be so silly. It didn't help.

I was utterly relieved to hear Aunt tell Mr. Sawaguchi we'd better go. I thanked him and said I was sorry, and we escaped into the lantern-lit street and the chatter of the crowds. A sickle moon was rising. It had stopped snowing.

攵

Chapter Eight

Back outside I felt better. Miki said she was hungry so we stopped at a stall to buy some chewy squid basted in soy sauce. The crowds had thickened and tea houses and coffee shops were doing good business.

"What happened in there, Hannah?" Aunt looked worried.

"She was frightened," said Hiro smugly.

I was so surprised to hear him speak, I almost dropped my squid. "He's right," I said. "I was frightened. I'm not sure why. I just felt so lonely."

"It's because you are a girl. Girls are not brave. Only boys."

I felt like whacking the self-satisfied little mushroom. Or saying something like, "Up your nose, Flower Boy." But I was too confused to think of the Japanese words. So I gave him a dirty look and turned my back, and as I did I heard the sound.

At first I thought it was the wind, whistling through tree branches, calling its winter song into the night sky. Or the cry of a wild bird. The clear rhythms echoed across the snowy darkness and danced in the firelight. I walked towards it without thinking.

The musician was not far away, standing under a lamp outside one of the coffeehouses. I'd never seen an instrument like the one he was playing. It was a long pipe made of brown, knotty wood. Except for his agile fingers moving up and down the pipe's stem, covering and uncovering its holes to draw out the music, he was very still. His face was shadowed by a deep basket-like hat made of woven straw. A black sash was looped around the shoulders of his dark kimono and he had a cloth bag slung from his waist. A wooden bowl lay in the snow beside his long, straw-sandaled feet. The small boy beside him reached just to his waist – a fat cherub in boots and a thick coat, he was holding a tray of tiny rice cakes, wrapped in thin paper, at a precarious angle.

"He's a monk of emptiness and nothingness," said Hiro's voice at my shoulder. "The instrument's called a *shakuhachi*."

I ignored him.

"A what?" asked Miki, coming up behind us, mouth full of squid.

"A wandering monk. In Edo times they earned their living by playing *shakuhachi* and spying for the government. If they played their *shakuhachi* softly, they could eavesdrop at the windows of houses at the same time. No one knew who they

56

were because of the hats. Of course this one isn't a real monk. He's playing a part for the festival."

"And how do you know about these monks?" said Miki.

Hiro looked at her as if to say he knew more than she'd ever know. What a pain in the neck!

"I am interested in history. And I read books, Mikiko. Long lines of writing. Made of paper."

Miki narrowed her eyes. I knew she wasn't a reader, and not especially good at schoolwork, and she didn't like having it pointed out.

"Real hilarious, Hiro. I'm going to buy more squid. Stay here with Hannah. I'll find Aunt Yukiyo."

The soft rich notes continued on. The monk who wasn't a monk stood deep in meditation, allowing the music to flow out of him. When at last he let the sound fade away, the crowd clapped gently. The monk slipped his *shakuhachi* into the cloth bag, picked up the bowl from the snowy ground and bowed his head. Lots of people went up and threw coins in the bowl. The little boy, bristling with importance, gave each of them a round cake.

Hiro dropped a five *yen* piece into the bowl and took his cake. Then it was my turn. The monk was very tall. I stood in his shadow and looked up, but I couldn't distinguish his face from the dark of the night.

"Where do you come from?" he asked suddenly. His voice was deep and syrupy, like warm honey.

"I'm from Australia."

"From Australia? You have come far to visit our city." He transferred the bowl to his left hand and, reaching into his left sleeve, pulled out a round object.

"Please take this," he said, putting it into my hands. "It has more meaning than a cake. Take it to your home. Its light will warm you. You will remember winter in Kanazawa as you watch its flame."

For a moment I stood speechless. Then I stepped closer to the light shed by the coffeehouse lamp so I could see better. The round thing was made of crinkly paper weathered to a pale-caramel color, and concertinaed almost flat. A piece of wood about the length of a chopstick was attached like a handle to one end. Inside, at its base, was a forked metal tongue. It was like nothing I'd ever seen and at the same time like something I remembered. What was it? I heard Hiro thank the player. When I looked up and tried to do the same, the player and the little boy had gone, and Hiro was waving to Aunt Yukiyo and Miki, who were pushing their way towards us through the crowds.

I showed them the concertina. "What is it, Aunt Yukiyo?" I asked.

Aunt Yukiyo took it in both hands. She pulled at the top end and extended it. It looked a bit like a small, round accordion.

"I think it's a sleeve lantern." She pointed inside. "You put your candle in and attach it to this fork. You hold it by the stick so its light shines in front of you. Your father will be fascinated, Miki. I wonder why the musician gave it to Hannah."

I was wondering that myself. I looked over to see what Miki thought. She was eyeing the lantern with a funny, preoccupied look on her face, as if she'd just remembered something.

夂

Chapter Nine

By the time we'd walked home to Kabuto Machi from the bus stop, I felt too tired to breathe. My face hurt from the cold and my mouth had gone numb.

"You're not accustomed to the snow yet," said Aunt Yukiyo. "You'll find it easier in a week or two."

Okaasan had hot tea waiting. Grateful to be out of the cold, I wrapped my hands hard around my tea bowl and sucked in the warmth. It even felt good to be sitting next to Granny, despite her drinking tea in loud slurps and gazing suspiciously at my feet. By the time Otōsan came home I was half asleep sitting up. He'd been out for a few beers with his friends.

We heard the shop door slam shut and some crashes, and then he came through to the living room, jovial and beaming. "Good evening. Good evening. How was the festival? And who's that boy on the stairs?"

We all looked at Hiro who was sitting drinking his tea. He wasn't the boy on the stairs. What other boys were there? Otōsan smiled rapturously and sank to the floor to join us. "Small boy. Wearing a samurai costume. Shaven head. Must be a wig. Friend of Hiro's?"

Okaasan and Aunt and Miki and Hiro and I leapt up and cannoned towards the stairs. Otōsan must have put Granny on her feet because she came scurrying after us. There were no small boys of any sort on the stairs, either in or out of samurai costume. We all trooped back to the table.

Granny smacked Otōsan on the back of his head. "Sozzled," she said. "Pickled. Disgraceful."

He looked sheepish and everyone laughed.

Five minutes later, upstairs in my room, I wasn't laughing. The smell hit me first, the unmistakable smell of summer and the beach. Sunscreen. My mother had insisted I bring some just in case we went skiing, or there was a sudden heat wave in the middle of the Japanese winter. Someone had taken my sunscreen and written *kanji* on my geisha mirror. And I knew what the *kanji* said. I recognized it as soon as I saw it, because I'd learned it that morning. *Umi.* The sea. What the heck was going on? Was Miki being funny? If it wasn't Miki, then who?

She wandered through the door covered in hair, like Cousin Itt from "The Addams Family." She stopped brushing and sniffed. "What's that funny smell?"

I pointed self-righteously at the mirror. "This is. Your parents are going to blame me, but I didn't do it. I didn't touch it. I haven't even been up here."

"Hooooo." Miki stared for a minute. Her face went pale and her eyes very black, and she muttered something to herself. "Come on," she said, her voice catching in her throat. She grabbed my arm and we went hurtling down the stairs. Ow! I bashed my elbow hard on the banister rail.

"Hey," I yelled, "we're not all athletic, you know. What are you doing?"

She ignored me, calling out, "Dad. Dad, where are you?"

He was in the kitchen, looking serene and other-worldly, making fresh tea.

"Dad, do you have that piece of paper from the yellow box?"

Otōsan smiled benevolently and wiggled a hand in the direction of the shop. "Under the counter."

We raced in, at least Miki raced and I followed, because I couldn't detach myself from her. She let me go while she fished around under the counter. I glared at the top of her head and massaged all my damaged joints. The orange lantern scattered light over the paper's fragile edges as she pulled it out of the box and flattened it on a space near the register, switching on the desk lamp so she could see. She read the first lines aloud.

If you, finder, choose to help the ocean boy,
Wait for the first snowfall.
The flute player at the temple of secrets
has the fox light.

62

"I knew it!" she exclaimed.

Then she started talking really fast. At first I had no idea what she was burbling about. I doubt if I could have understood even if she was speaking English, because she was so agitated that all her words were running together. My mother would have diagnosed OVEREXCITEMENT. But gradually I began to understand. Then I wished I hadn't.

"Hannah, don't you see? He gave you the fox light. The sleeve lantern is the fox light. Travelers lit them in olden times to chase away fox spirits on the roads. The *shakuhachi* player gave it to you. The Ninja Temple is the temple of secrets. And the first snow is falling." She waved the paper at me, tapped it with a teacherly finger. "It's … this is coming true."

"So a *shakuhachi* is …"

"A flute. A bamboo flute."

"I thought it was a recorder."

"Think, Hannah. The *kanji* on your mirror. *Umi*, the sea. Or *Kai*. You can read it as *Kai*. *Kai* is a boy's name. A boy named for the ocean. The ocean boy." She paused. Her face changed. I could almost see the light bulb flashing on in her brain. "The boy Dad saw on the stairs. I bet it's him."

"The samurai boy? There wasn't anyone there! Besides, your father's a bit … well, you know … not himself tonight. I mean Miki, great balls of fire, it's crazy. You don't seriously think your father's seeing ghosts, do you?"

"That is exactly what I think," she said. "It's not the first time. Dad's seen ghosts before. They seem to like him. Don't

63

mention it to him, he gets very embarrassed. He doesn't like THEM at all. There's something about him and Aunt, you see, something that attracts magic. And you heard what Mum said about the shadows in Kanazawa winters."

"Yeeees. The shadows. But … but …" I gaped at Miki's excited face, not sure if I was hearing right.

"I think we're the finders," she continued, "and we're being asked to help the ocean boy. How else do you explain the *kanji* on your mirror? If you didn't write it and I didn't write it, who did? Mum? Dad? Granny?"

I wouldn't have put it past Granny but I didn't say that. I couldn't deny something weird was happening. The flower cards flew around the stairs for no reason and my mother fell down there. A musician gave me a lantern and someone wrote *kanji* on my mirror. And Miki's father had seen a little samurai on the stairs who wasn't there two minutes later.

"Um … I don't know who could have written it. This is so crazy! I don't like ghosts. I don't even believe in ghosts! And what could we do to help anyway?"

"I don't know. We need to think. I'll take this paper with me. Dad won't miss it. On second thought I'll take the toy box too."

We turned off the shop lights and climbed back up the stairs, not saying a word. We were both thinking very hard.

That night I dreamt again. I was in a tunnel. My head was crushed against the roof, so I had to crouch. It was dark as pitch and bitterly cold. I smelled dank fish and fear and blood. Echoes like hissing voices ran along the icy slime on the walls. Water rushed through the echoes but I couldn't tell what direction it came from. Once my eyes adjusted to the dark, I could see, but my mouth and nose were covered with material and I could barely breathe. A scream was rising in my throat when I saw the light.

It was just a pinpoint in the distance, but panic ran across my nerve endings like ice water. Someone was coming towards me. If this was an enemy I was finished. The light came closer and I flattened myself against the wall and squeezed my eyelids shut. Yellow light very close. *Open your eyes, Hannah.*

It was only a child, a small boy with a cushiony face and the front part of his head shaven. He smiled and took my hand, and led me forward into the dark by the light of his lantern.

夂

Chapter Ten

I slept in the next morning and woke up thick-headed and grumpy. I couldn't think what day it was. Monday? No, it had to be Tuesday. Where was the clock? Nine already. Miki would have gone to school. In daylight I couldn't believe she was serious about the ghost. The idea that a little samurai had come from the past to visit us was bizarre. I looked out the window to a dull sky and peevish rain melting the snow in the garden. I felt peevish and dull too.

On the floor outside my bedroom door I found a neat plastic package. Okaasan had left a school uniform for me. I tried it on and went to stand in front of my geisha mirror. The sea *kanji* was still there, pinkish-beige and set hard – Miki hadn't wanted me to clean it off. I couldn't see my head and face properly, but what I could see was enough. The uniform was too long and too tight. Its cut didn't flatter my squareness and the crimson sailor collar clashed horribly with my hair. I looked like Attila the Hun dressed as Barbie. And I had to go out in public wearing it tomorrow. I yanked it off in such a hurry I caught a thread on the charm bracelet I always wore. Darn. I threw on my tracksuit and ran downstairs.

I opened the shop door and stuck my head through to say good morning.

"*Ohayō gozaimasu*," said a crackly voice.

Granny beamed at me from her blue chair. She was munching a donut from a blue and white takeout box on her lap. Aunt Yukiyo must have brought them in. Otōsan was pottering, pale and fragile, in the Old Corner. He nodded to me, but I think it hurt him to move his head.

I went to the kitchen looking for some breakfast. Okaasan was at a recycling meeting till twelve, so I had to get my own.

I glanced out the window. The rain had stopped and a gauze-like mist was drifting across the garden. I felt cocooned inside its softness, separate and safe, but a bit lonely, too. I wondered what my family would be doing. I tried to picture them. Liana would be torturing gardeners in Tokyo. Dad would probably be in the sun at Opal Street Station, waiting for the train to work. Joel, with luck, had been abducted by aliens.

Weather-wise, it was a morning for porridge or sausages or hot chocolate, but I decided on toast and honey. Then I couldn't find the toaster or the honey, so I had to settle for plain bread and butter. Which gave me the galloping grouches, as my dad would say.

It wasn't that I didn't like bread and butter. At home on summer mornings Dad and I always got up early. He made tea and cut slices of fresh bread. I lathered them with butter. We had to have our bread and butter early, so Liana didn't see. We weren't allowed butter. She made us eat Healthy Harry's Super Spread (salt-reduced, cholesterol free). But even if she did catch us, it didn't usually matter, because Dad just gave her a big cuddle and told her that she was funny and clever and the best thing since sliced bread. She liked him saying that, I don't know why. Sliced bread is way down on my list of things I'd like to be compared to!

I supposed Hiro missed doing fun things with his dad. Maybe they used to go fishing or camping together. Then I wondered about our ocean boy. I was certain he wasn't hanging around like Miki said, but if he was, where was his family? Even *if* he was a ghost, he was still a little kid. Why was he here alone? For that matter, why was he here at all?

I washed up my plate. Thinking I might walk to the river to cheer myself up, I put on boots and took an umbrella and went outside. But it was cold and wet and miserable, and walking by myself didn't help at all.

Back in the house, it was chilly and dark. The shop didn't open till ten so there were no customers yet, only Otōsan and his headache and Granny and her donuts. I decided to go up to my room, collect my books and bring them back to the kitchen. If I turned on the light and the heater, it would be cozy. I was certain Miki's ghost theory was pure hogwash but I

68

just didn't fancy being up in my room alone.

I almost put my foot on the Banana Dream. It lay squashed into a creamy mess on the bottom step, as if someone had taken a baseball bat to it. Granny must have dropped it. I picked it up with two fingers and took it to the kitchen bin. Then I found a rag, went back, wiped up the leftover goo, rinsed out the rag and started up the stairs again.

On the second to last step I found another donut – a Screaming Strawberry, shell-pink ooze dripping from squashed fruit. It looked as if someone had jumped up and down on it for fun. I stomped back down to the kitchen for the rag. Why should I have to clean up Granny's mess? My face was hot with annoyance. I was glad of the breeze on the stairs ruffling my hair.

Back in my room I gathered up an armful – *kanji* book, dictionaries, pencil case, notebook, and the brown correspondence envelope. I slipped the flower cards into my pocket. Maybe I'd take a look at them during a study break. I ducked to catch an escaping pencil and happened to glance in the mirror. Was that red bird's nest my hair? I'd forgotten to brush it. It was tangled and sticking up. I had to put everything down again and that made me mad. I grabbed a handful of tissues and scrubbed the *kanji* off the mirror. I needed to see what I was doing. Miki would have to understand. I brushed and brushed and got even madder. My hair still looked like an intoxicated porcupine. I felt like throwing things. I slammed the brush down and loaded up

69

my books again. Patted my pocket to check on the cards. Near the door I stumbled and dropped my dictionary. Gingerly bending down to pick it up, so I wouldn't drop everything else, I happened to glance again in the mirror. My face should have been there. It wasn't. Something else was. Something unexpected and shocking and really, really scary.

The cards fell from my pocket and slapped down on the floor. I left them. I flew out the door and along the corridor and down the stairs at breakneck speed. I was halfway down when a donut whizzed past my ear and splattered on the wall beside me. Chocolate syrup sprayed across my face and into one eye. I lost my footing and slid and bumped to the bottom of the stairs on my backside. Books scattered everywhere. My charm bracelet flew off my wrist.

The sliding doors to the shop shot open and Otōsan's alarmed face poked through. "Oooh. Oooh." he said. "Oooh."

It seemed to be his standard remark for surprising situations. I guessed he was wondering if Australians spent all their time falling down stairs.

I was in no condition to explain.

I apologized – *"Gomen nasai!"* – and told him I was fine, all the time grabbing at my books, listening to the booming of my heart and licking off the chocolate running down my chin. Where was the bracelet? Otōsan picked it up from between his feet and I shoved it in my pocket. As soon as he would let me I sprinted through the kitchen, out the garden door into the lane, around the corner and in through the door of the

Honey House.

I don't often sprint and I was puffing like a steam train as I cannoned into Toshi, Aunt Yukiyo's assistant. Toshi had hair almost the same color as mine, but his was dyed. He sat me at a table as far as possible from the other customers and went to the kitchen to call Aunt, who came hurrying out to sit with me.

"Don't try to talk, Hannah. I can see you've had a fright."

Toshi brought me a hot chocolate. I said no thanks to a donut; I was already wearing one. The chocolate was warm and sweet in my throat. Aunt Yukiyo came gradually into focus. I noticed she was wearing an apron with jars of honey all over it, dangly bee earrings and silver sparkles around her eyes.

"Can you tell me what's wrong, Hannah?" she said gently.

I took a gulp of air. "It must have happened because I wiped off the *kanji*. I shouldn't have touched it. Okaasan isn't home, and I didn't think Granny or Otōsan would understand, so I came here. Miki says you know about mysterious happenings because you lived on the Shimo-something Peninsula. I thought you might know what to do." I paused, out of breath.

Aunt Yukiyo wrinkled her forehead. She didn't need to tell me I wasn't making sense. "Why not start from the beginning, Hannah?" she said. "Tell me everything. Slowly."

It's hard to think in a second language when you're having a nervous breakdown, but I got my story out. I told her about the yellow box and the toys and the message on the square paper. About the *kanji* on the mirror and Miki's ghost theory, about the squashed donuts and the Chocolate Surprise

71

attacking me on the stairs. And what I'd seen in the mirror.

Aunt nodded and made encouraging noises, but didn't speak. When I'd finished, she sucked her breath in through her teeth, tilting her head so her thick ponytail swung from side to side. "A little ghost in the house," she said. "Remarkable. Now tell me again about the mirror."

"I bent down to pick up my dictionary. I looked in the mirror and my face wasn't there. There was a ship. A ship with tall square sails. Dark waves were crashing around it. I could HEAR the waves, Aunt Yukiyo. And it was snowing. There was a kind of white haze running down the mirror."

A dreamy look crossed Aunt Yukiyo's face. "It must have been quite beautiful." Then she frowned, concentrating. "So Miki thinks the ocean boy is a samurai child named Kai. A naughty child it seems, if he's vandalizing Granny's donuts. A child with a connection to a ship or ships. And according to the paper you found, he needs help. But you don't know what kind of help he needs and you don't know why."

"Aunt Yukiyo," I said, "Aren't you taking all this a bit calmly? If this is a ghost, shouldn't we be doing a tiny bit of PANICKING?"

Aunt smiled and shook her head, so that the bees on her earrings jiggled in an irritating, carefree kind of way.

"No panicking is necessary, Hannah. He's just a child from a different time, asking for help. Don't you think it's important to help whenever you can, even if the situation is a bit unusual?"

72

A BIT unusual? I slumped down in my seat and sighed.

"I do, but …" Suddenly I felt really tired and the right words wouldn't come. I truly didn't mind helping. People, that was.

Aunt Yukiyo patted my hand. "Hannah," she went on, "I want you to eat something for me. It's a new kind of donut I've been working on. It's made with medicinal herbs and green tea and it's very strengthening. You've had some nasty shocks and I think it would do you good."

She didn't wait for an answer. "Toshi *san*," she called, "could you bring Hannah a Gorgeous Green Glacier?"

The plate Toshi put in front of me held an iced green donut flecked with what looked like bits of grass. I took a cautious bite. The dough was warm, with a sweet fizzy taste, and filled with a river of green tea ice cream. As I ate I could feel myself relax. The acrobat inside my stomach stopped tumbling.

"Now," said Aunt, "when Miki comes home we'll need to talk to her and make a plan. Can you remember the next line of the message?"

I shut my eyes and tried to remember Otōsan's voice in the shop three nights ago. "'At the hour of the bull bring the light to the shrine where women go to poison the hearts of their rivals.'"

"'The shrine where women go to poison the hearts of their rivals?'" repeated Aunt. "I don't think I've ever heard of such a place. Perhaps one of the guide books will have some information. Now, let's go next door and clean up. Then you can study here for the rest of the morning and later we'll make some lunch. Remember, tomorrow's your first day at school. That's important too."

Chapter Eleven

I didn't feel too pleased to see Hiro waiting for us outside the flower shop the next morning, wearing street clothes and his grey parka, spiky hair hidden under a baseball cap. I didn't like his attitude one bit. He was standing ramrod straight with a purposeful expression on his face, like a mushroom concentrating. It turned out he was concentrating on being friendly.

"Good morning, Hannah and Miki," he said in English. "It's nice to see you."

Could Hiro be thawing? I took a chance and asked him why he was in street clothes. He said primary schoolers usually wore street clothes to school. I said I hadn't realized he was still in primary school. He seemed really old. Maybe I'd feel old, too, if my dad disappeared.

During the night the temperature had plummeted. The rain had gone and snow was falling intermittently. Icicles hung from underneath bridges and the willow trees along the riverbank were delicate sculptures of frosted white. I clumped along in my sailor uniform and Okaasan's boots. I had buttoned my coat to the neck so the crimson collar wouldn't clash with my hair. Maybe I should have gone to primary school with Hiro. Then I could have worn street clothes too.

Hiro walked with us to his school's gate and said a solemn goodbye. We went on down the road. Lots of other kids were walking in the same direction, and boys in black trousers and black jackets fastened to the neck with gold buttons whizzed past us on bikes. A bus jam-packed with school kids rumbled by.

I was too young for Miki's class. We both had birthdays in September but I'd turned twelve and she'd turned thirteen. She told me Hiro was two months younger than me. He'd be starting junior high at the beginning of the new school year in March. My mother said my age was IRRELEVANT. Nobody would expect me to actually LEARN anything at junior high. I was going there for the LIFE EXPERIENCE and the *KANJI*. At the time I'd thought it made sense, but if I'd known how bad I'd look in the uniform I'd have put up a fight.

The junior high was a rectangular cement block near the river. A snow covered playing field stretched beside it. At the student entrance Miki showed me the First Years' shoe box. I took off my boots, placed them neatly in the box and put on a new pair of sneakers that I'd brought to use as my indoor school shoes. From now on I'd leave them at school permanently.

"We'll go to the staffroom first," said Miki. "I have to introduce you to the Deputy Principal and to Miss Ida. You'll be in 1B with me, so Miss Ida will be your homeroom teacher. She's our Japanese teacher too."

In the staffroom were two long rows of desks piled high with books and papers. The teachers sat behind them, writing or working on their word processors. The Deputy Principal was perched behind a table at one end of the room, like a supervisor. As we walked towards him some of the teachers looked up and smiled and nodded. That made me feel warm inside and a bit less nervous. The Deputy Principal didn't smile. He was poker-faced and smelled of onions. He asked me lots of questions, but I could tell he wasn't the least bit interested in the answers. Miss Ida was dainty and young, with serious glasses and short bobbed hair. She looked as if she should still have been in high school.

After we got away from the Deputy Principal, Miki showed me the rest of the school. Lots of kids glanced at me curiously, some smiled, some stared, and two older boys looked me up and down and laughed. I didn't know if it was my face or my uniform they were laughing at, but they made me feel self-conscious and a bit depressed.

Miki glared at them. "That's Kenjiro Kamogawa and his stupid friend, Riki," she said. "They're Third Years and they're brainless bullying idiots. The best way to deal with them is to pretend they don't exist."

I thought the best way to deal with them might be a punch in the head, but I kept that to myself.

The toilets and the gym were on the ground floor and there were two floors of classrooms above. I was surprised we were allowed to go up to our classroom without a teacher. We hung our coats in the corridor outside 1B's classroom and put our umbrellas in the rack.

"Come on," said Miki. "I'll introduce you." I took a deep breath and followed her in.

There were about thirty-five desks and chairs in rows facing the blackboard. Kids were chatting or studying or finishing their homework. A square stove stood in the center of the room. From the stove a bronze-colored pipe ran up and across the ceiling and out a hole in the wall. On top of the stove there was a round tin bowl of water with chunks of ice floating in it.

"The stove heats the room," Miki explained, "and the water in the bowl keeps the air moist. Sometimes the water freezes if the nights are very cold, but the room heats up quickly once the stove has been lit. Sometimes it gets too hot. You'll see. Miss Ida thought you should sit next to it because you'll be feeling the cold more than anyone else. This is your desk."

I sat down and fiddled with my pencil case, feeling silly. Miki brought her friends, Chiharu and Yuka and a boy called Shin, over to meet me. Two of her other friends were at home, sick with winter flu. Yuka had heard on the news that the government was concerned there might be a flu epidemic. Shin said the principal was home sick, and that Mrs. Ogawa, the teacher in charge of the Third Years, was in the hospital with a lung infection. When the chimes sounded for the beginning of lessons there were ten students missing from 1B.

The most nerve-wracking time for me was at the beginning of the first lesson, which was Math. Mr. Sekita, the teacher, came in at eight forty-five and everyone in the class stood up and bowed to him. I got a shock when he asked me to introduce myself formally to the class. For a few seconds I panicked and couldn't think what to say. But then I remembered my speech.

I'd won the Primary Japanese Speech Contest in Year Six, coming first in the whole of Brisbane. So I said, "*Minasan Hajimemashite.*" That means "How do you do, everyone." Then I said, "*Watashi wa Hannah desu.*" Only I pronounced Hannah as "Ha Na," so it would be easy for the kids to remember. The rest of my speech went like this.

"*Juu ni sai desu.*" I'm twelve.

"*Oosutoraria jin desu.*" I'm Australian.

"*Kazoku ga yonin imasu.*" There are four people in my family.

"*Inu o katte imasu.*" I have a dog.

"*Terebi o miru koto ga suki desu.*" I like watching TV.

"*Supootsu wa nettobooru o shimasu.*" I play netball.

"*Yoroshiku onegai shimasu.*" Very pleased to meet you.

I found out afterwards that nobody understood about the netball because Japanese girls don't play it. But the class smiled and clapped, and I hoped they might like me, despite the uniform.

Chapter Twelve

When my performance was over I settled down to vegetate at my desk. I listened to Mr. Sekita's voice floating and circling through the warm air of the room and did what I could of the math problems. Mostly I watched the snow falling past the square windows.

After Math came Science, and then double Japanese. Each lesson was fifty minutes long. After every lesson there was a ten minute break when we could talk or go to the toilet or have a drink. I went to the toilet after Science. When I went into the cubicle I found what looked like a small hand basin set into the floor. Big panic. I'd never used a Japanese-style toilet before. The Maekawas had one Western-style, one Japanese. It took me so long to figure out what to do I almost missed the start of the Japanese lesson.

Miss Ida started out teaching *kanji*. She gave us some

combinations to write out. That was easy. Then we had to read a story and answer questions. Much more difficult. I only got one answer right.

Around eleven-thirty my stomach started screeching that it wanted morning tea. Then the heat from the stove began to make me sleepy. I had to prop my eyes open with my fingers. The boy on the opposite side of the stove was fast asleep, head on his desk and mouth wide open. Nobody woke him up and Miss Ida ignored him. I was astonished. I could imagine the reaction of Mrs. Battersby, my Year Seven teacher, if she'd found me asleep during one of her lessons. She'd have made me stay in at lunch to finish the work I'd slept through, then she'd have hot-footed it to the telephone and asked my parents if they thought I was taking drugs.

Miki was on the roster for lunch duty with five others. Miss Ida told me to go with them. I think she was fed up with watching me yawn. We left ten minutes before the end of class, washed our hands, and put on aprons and plastic shower cap hats. It wasn't a good look but it did keep your hair out of other people's food. Truck drivers from the School Lunch Center were waiting downstairs to hand over large metal containers of food. I was allowed to wheel one of the trolleys back to the stairs.

Back in the classroom we put bowls and plates on twenty-seven lunch trays and dished out the food – pork and vegetable soup, fish balls, potato salad, a carton of milk each. Everyone brought their own rice. Miki and I had ours in plastic lunchboxes, but some of the kids had aluminum containers and they'd put them on the stove to heat. The warming rice gave off a mouthwatering, grainy smell. I was ravenous. At home I kept mini Mars Bars in my schoolbag for emergency hunger attacks, but Miki told me that being caught eating a chocolate bar at her school created a major drama. It was SO against the rules. So I gave the Mars Bars a miss. I didn't need a major drama.

Miss Ida was a bit late coming back for lunch and we couldn't say "*itadakimasu*" and start eating until she arrived. She didn't look too excited. She probably didn't want to eat with a bunch of grotty kids. I wouldn't, if I was a teacher. Mrs. Battersby wouldn't even let you put your nose in the staff room to give her a message during lunchtime. She said she saw enough of us in the classroom and if she saw any more she'd have a nervous breakdown. You couldn't dislodge Mrs. B. from that staffroom at lunchtime if you blew it up. She'd be sitting in the rubble eating her sandwiches and her yogurt and drinking coffee.

Miki's friend Chiharu didn't want her potato salad and a boy called Takuro didn't want his fish balls, so I ate those as well as my own. While Miki helped clean up, I went down to the gym with Yuja and Shin. It was crowded and smelled of moist feet and the insides of sneakers. We watched the Second Years play basketball and I asked Shin what we'd be doing in Music and English in the afternoon. Choir practice in Music, grammar in English. I liked to sing and English was a breeze, so the afternoon flew past. But the most fun was cleaning.

Japanese schools don't employ cleaners. The kids do the cleaning themselves. When I think of Billy Thompson, who I sat next to in Year Seven, I think it's a great idea. He was such a pig. Every day he'd drop pencil shavings and bits of shredded paper and candy wrappers under his desk. He never picked any of his rubbish up unless Mrs. Battersby spotted him and yelled. "It's the cleaner's job," he'd say. Smarmy little turkey. It would have done him SO much good if he'd had to clean up his mess himself. Better yet if he'd had to clean the toilets. If I'd been in charge I'd definitely have made him clean the toilets. Preferably with his head.

Adult cleaners probably do a better job than kids. Miki and Chiharu and I were on first floor corridors. We had the best time. First we put our cleaning rags on the floor, one under each hand. We charged up and down the corridors on our hands and feet until the floors were ice rink slippery. Then we tried skateboarding on our rags. I couldn't say if the corridors were clean when we finished but I knew they were shiny.

Miki didn't have basketball club on Wednesdays so we walked home together.

"No Hiro this afternoon?" I asked.

"I usually only see him in the mornings," Miki answered. "Sometimes he goes to cram school in the afternoons. Or to see his mother."

"Where is she?"

"She works out near the airport. She lives there most of

the time, rents a room. She's a taxi driver. When Hiro's father didn't phone or write and they couldn't trace him, she said she needed to earn some money to support herself and Hiro. Grandpa Honda offered to take care of them, but she wouldn't hear of it. Hiro's been cross and miserable ever since it happened. He can't live with his mum because her hours aren't regular. He gets on well with his granddad but they'd both like their family back together."

So there were good reasons why Hiro was a pain in the neck.

"What do you think happened to his father?"

Miki tipped her head to one side, thinking. "Hiro's father is an entomologist and last spring he went to Yonaguni Island. It's tiny, far down in the southwest. He was on a field trip with some other scientists, researching these huge orange and green moths that live there. Hiro says they're as big as Western dinner plates. The trip only lasted a month, but Hiro's dad never came home. They know he hired a boat from a fisherman on Yonaguni and set off north by himself. Then he just vanished. I think he must have drowned, but Hiro suspects he's run off and left them, and that makes losing his father twice as bad."

I resolved to be much nicer to Hiro. I knew he must feel terrible. My dad was only as far away as the phone, and I still missed him heaps. But when we came through the doors of the Mulberry Tree I forgot Hiro, because I thought I was seeing things. Mobile Phone was at the counter. I could tell it was him by the unusual shape of his head and the red phone.

Miki didn't know about Mobile Phone so she walked straight past him, but I had a good look. Up close he was stunningly handsome, like an older Ricky Martin. Broad shoulders and sparkly eyes and thick black hair with grey tips.

We almost missed the juiciness of what happened next because we were halfway into the house when Otōsan came to serve him. And Mobile Phone spoke so softly we could barely hear.

"It's been a long time, Maekawa *san*. We knew each other many years ago. I am Kiminori Shimizu and I have come hoping for news of your sister, Yukiyo."

I heard Miki gasp and she grabbed my arm. We gaped at each other. Aunt Yukiyo's KimiShimi! He was back. And he was gorgeous.

We saw Otōsan give a quick, shallow bow. His face was cold and his voice crisp. It was like watching warm water transform itself into an iceberg. "I remember you well, Shimizu *san*. The memory is not a happy one. My sister no longer lives in this house. Good afternoon."

No mention of Aunt living right next door! Otōsan turned away and after a moment so did KimiShimi. Miki and I slid out of the shop and went through to the kitchen, stunned into silence.

Granny was perched near the window. "A message from Yukiyo," she crackled. "You're to go in and see her as soon as you've changed."

夂
Chapter Thirteen

The Honey House was crammed with noisy groups of school kids, university students, middle-aged ladies taking a break from shopping, a few men in suits, and some American and German tourists who'd come in to shelter from the cold. They crowded around its tables sipping coffee and chocolate and hot tea, and munching on mountains of donuts.

Aunt Yukiyo was behind the counter serving a young German woman. She beckoned us over. "I don't have time to explain now," she said to us, "but I want you to eat dinner at my house tonight. I've seen your mother, Miki, and it's all arranged. Get your homework done and come over at seven. You'll probably be staying the night, so bring your toothbrushes and pajamas. And some warm clothes, coats, gloves, thick socks and hats. And bring the sleeve lantern. See you later." She turned back to her customer. "Would you like your cinnamon swirls warmed up, madam?"

Miki and I looked at each other in astonishment. Why would we need all that stuff to spend the night in a heated house? And why were we going there at all?

Back upstairs above the Mulberry Tree I stood at Miki's door, watching her spread her schoolbooks out on the floor around her.

"What did you think of KimiShimi?" I asked.

Miki grinned and made pop eyes. "He's spectacular. Almost as beautiful as Aunt. Dad wasn't very friendly though, was he?"

"He was a frosticle. Are you going to tell Aunt Yukiyo that KimiShimi's looking for her?"

"I'd like to. I'd like to see her face when she hears. Do you think I should?"

"I'm not sure," I said. "Otōsan must have a good reason for not wanting her to know."

"I suppose. I'll think about it. We don't want her racing off to Aomori again." She opened her history book. "You're so lucky not having to do homework, Hannah. Do you want to help me answer these questions?"

"Would I be any help? No, I think I'll go and have a bath. I feel like soaking and thinking. My head's going to explode if it has to cope with any more information today."

I went next door to my room to pick up some fresh clothes.

I glanced at the mirror, saw with relief that it was empty of everything but my short, uniformed self and bits of my room. No ships tossing or waves crashing.

"I'm sooo jealous," Miki had wailed when I'd told her. "Why can't I see something? Anything would do!"

"Are you crazy?" I'd answered. "I almost fainted with fright. And even when I got outside, donuts came pitching at me like cricket balls! It was extremely nerve-racking!"

I collected underclothes and thermal socks, warm sweatpants, two wool sweaters and my toiletry bag, and put them in a carry basket on my table. Okaasan had left a fresh towel rolled up beside the basket. What a honey. My mother made me get my own towels. I peeked again at the mirror. My squashed-up face was where it should be. Good! Only, was I feeling just a teeny bit disappointed that everything was so normal?

My flower cards were on the table next to my *kanji* book, which was open at the "nature" page where I'd left it. I ran my eyes over the shapes. Sky, rain, cloud, snow, sea, mountain, thunder, wind. Yep, I had them engraved on my brain. That meant I knew thirty-eight *kanji* and had nine hundred and sixty-two to learn. Not that I was counting.

I picked up the flower cards and shuffled them. Miki was going to teach me to play as soon as she had time. Shuffle, shuffle, miss. Shuffling wasn't my thing. I always dropped at least one. I looked at the picture. It was pretty, a green and gold bird surrounded by crimson plum blossoms. I stuck it back in the pack. Shuffle, shuffle, miss again. Bummer. I'd dropped the same card.

I imagined myself glamorous and gorgeous and much taller, slinking into a casino. Maybe I'd be wearing a red dress. Something sparkly. Well, maybe not red, not with my hair. Silver then. Brad Pitt would be there at a table and I'd sashay right up to him and whip out my personal deck of cards.

"Pick a card, Brad. Any card."

And Brad would pick his card and on it would be … a green-gold bird surrounded by plum blossoms. Again? I stared at the card I'd pulled out of the pack. The bird perched regally on its forked branch. I'd turned it up three times in a row. This was too weird. See ya, Brad. I took my things in their carry basket and headed downstairs.

In the bathroom I shut and latched the door. I put my fresh clothes ready on a shelf, took off the dirty ones and placed them on the shelf underneath. Then I stepped down into the bathroom and settled my backside on a plastic stool near the wall taps. Using a handheld shower hose I washed myself thoroughly with white soap and washed my hair. Steam filled the little room.

When I'd hosed off every molecule of grease and dirt and soap suds, I rolled the bath cover back and sank chin deep into piping hot water. Granny bathed first in the family, at five every afternoon. She always put herbal powder in her bath and liked the water scalding. So did I, despite looking like a freshly cooked lobster when I got out. I hadn't liked the idea of sharing bath water with other people at first, and especially not with Granny. But once I realized that everyone who got into that water was squeaky clean, I didn't mind.

I lay there for about fifteen minutes, letting my mind wander. Images of Mr. Sekita teaching Math and the Ninja Temple under snow and KimiShimi in the shop and flying donuts on the stairs ran through my brain at random. I breathed in hot, herb-scented steam. When I couldn't take the heat any longer I stepped out of the water, rolling the bath cover back over to keep the water hot for the next person. Reaching for my towel, I wondered what the night would bring.

Aunt Yukiyo had made *sushi* and *tempura*.

"According to Granny," she said when we were settled at the table, "the shrine where women went in olden times to poison the hearts of their rivals is Sarumaru Jinja. Sarumaru Shrine. I should have remembered. It's on the new Saigawa Road. A woman who thought her husband was cheating on her would pray there for illness or death to strike down the other woman. Now we have divorce and the shrine is not much used. But if you want to help Kai I think it's important you go there tonight. I'll drive you."

We had to go TONIGHT? The bath had made me warm and sleepy, and it was snowing again. It would be freezing outside! I got grumpy just thinking about it. "I wish we'd never found that piece of paper!"

"But you did find it, Hannah, you and Miki. You can't change that!"

Aunt Yukiyo took a battered prawn in her chopsticks. I watched her glumly. She looked so lovely. She cooked like an angel. Why was she dragging innocent and fragile children out in arctic temperatures to help nasty, donut-lobbing ghosts?

"We could put it back," I said. "That'd save a lot of trouble."

Aunt poured three bowls of tea. "You could, Hannah. Putting the paper back would be the easy way out. But the easy way isn't always a good choice. Kai needs you to follow this through. He must have been very young when he died, but still there's something he couldn't finish or that he needs to know. For a reason about which I have no clue, you're the ones who are able to help him finish his story."

"Besides," said Miki, "he'll probably just keep chucking donuts at you till we do."

Aunt shot Miki a stern look. "And you're right, Hannah, it is a bitter night, much better spent indoors. But we don't have time to wait for a better one. Tomorrow is the fourth of February, *Setsubun*."

Miki slapped herself on the head. "Of course. I hadn't thought."

"What's *Setsubun*?"

"The bean throwing festival," said Miki. "And according to the message, we should get the talisman before the bean throwing. Otherwise the rest won't fall into place. Tonight may be our only chance. So we should wash the dishes and get some sleep."

I was confused. "Why do we have to get some sleep? Why can't we just go now?"

"Because," said Aunt Yukiyo, "we have to go to the shrine at the hour of the bull. Two in the morning. That's why I asked you to stay."

"Two in the MORNING?"

She woke us with hot tea at one. We rugged up in coats and gloves and hats and padded out to the street where her car was parked. The city was white and silent, bathed in icy moonlight. It had stopped snowing but was bitterly cold. I had matches and a candle in my coat pocket. Miki was carrying the sleeve lantern in a plastic shopping bag.

We drove along the route we'd followed in the bus, but instead of going straight over the Saigawa Bridge we turned left at the Katamachi intersection. After that I lost my bearings in a maze of twists and turns. Sitting mesmerized in the back seat, I wondered if I was dreaming. Was I really driving around Kanazawa at one-thirty in the morning with two people I'd only just met, searching for a talisman that might help a boy who'd lived maybe centuries ago? Miki had said there was something magic about her aunt and her father. I figured she must have inherited the trait. She didn't seem to be finding all this the least bit bizarre.

Aunt Yukiyo parked under a streetlight. The road was wide and neon lit, empty except for an occasional car cruising past. We trod up the path to the ancient shrine. Immense cherry trees with snow encrusted along their branches stood stark against the ebony sky.

"Now what?" whispered Miki.

"Why are you whispering?" asked Aunt. "And stop rattling that bag. Let's light the lantern."

I pulled the candle from my coat pocket and cupped my right hand around the wick. Miki struck a match and the flame flowered in the dark. Aunt Yukiyo took the candle from me and slid it inside the lantern, catching it securely in the metal teeth. Then she lifted it high, letting the light wander across the trees. High on their trunks we could see scars, like the marks of nails. Our breath came in misty clouds. We waited in silence. I felt the cold creeping across my skin and inside my head.

A clock struck far away behind us in the city center. Chimes rang through the crisp air. One. Two. It was the hour of the bull. Air seemed to shift and the lantern light shuddered, and in a breath the Saigawa Road and its neon vanished, plunging us into sightless, blood-chilling darkness. I don't remember ever being so frightened.

"The matches, Miki?" Aunt Yukiyo's voice was calm. There was a soft hiss and the smells of sap and wax. Aunt's face hovered, spectral, above the flame, and the sleeve lantern's light blossomed again into a small comforting glow.

My heart slowed. As my eyes became accustomed to the semi-darkness, I saw paddy fields stretching away from us in every direction, bitter-white and barren. Fearfully I noticed that the nail scars on the trunks of the cherry trees were no longer above my head but directly in front of my eyes. Bitumen and cement had gone; the trees were younger. Suddenly I understood I was seeing Sarumaru Jinja in a time that wasn't my own.

A rustling of silk and the tap-tap of wooden sandals. We huddled together in the lantern's pool of light. The woman who came down the shrine path was small and angular. Thin wrists protruded from the sleeves of her white kimono. Her black hair was loose on her shoulders and in her mouth she carried a comb, its teeth protruding towards us. She gave no sign she knew we were there but tapped past us to stand before the trunk of the largest cherry, running pale fingers across its bark as if searching for the right place. She rested her palm flat against the trunk.

None of us moved. We watched, astonished, fear rippling across our silence.

She turned then, scrutinized us with cold eyes. Searching. The straw doll she pulled from her kimono sleeve was crudely made and about as long as her hand. Taking the comb from between her teeth, she slipped it into her sleeve and spoke.

"Bring the lantern closer."

A voice like a dentist's drill. We crept towards her and Aunt lifted the lantern so its light fell on the tree trunk. The woman took a hammer and a long nail from her sleeve. She placed the point of the nail against the doll's heart and the

95

hammering began. It echoed across empty fields, falling down to the snow and ringing across the sky. We stood frozen, hypnotized by the rhythm, watching the lantern light flutter across her white hands. Hammer clanged against metal as she drove the nail through the doll's heart and into the tree. I couldn't drag my eyes away, much as I wanted to. Her straw doll had red-brown hair, the same color as mine.

She finished, sighed a satisfied malicious sigh, then reached back into her sleeve for the comb. It was exquisite, black lacquer work in the shape of a half circle. She held it up in front of her face, staring at us through the teeth.

"*Kushi*," she said in her whiny voice. "A comb. *Ku. Shi.* Do you know your numbers, foreigner?"

I nodded. Couldn't speak. My voice was trapped somewhere down near my toes. I was lucky I could get my head to move.

"*Ku*, nine, for suffering. *Shi*, four, for death. Take the comb. Take it as you took my life away from me." She held it out.

What did she mean, I took her life away? I didn't want to touch her comb. I'd rather have picked up a death adder. But perhaps I had to?

"Take it, Hannah," urged Miki. "Quickly! It must be the talisman."

"No. No, Hannah, don't touch it. The comb is evil. It's not the talisman." Aunt's hand was on my arm.

The woman turned her gaze to Aunt Yukiyo. Her eyes glowed black as gleaming sword tips and just as dangerous.

"You think yourself clever, you born on the night of deep snow. Give me the lantern."

Yuki, snow. *Yo*, night. I hadn't realized. Aunt Yukiyo's name meant Snowy Night. She held out the lantern stick and Comb-Teeth took it. I held my breath.

Aunt Yukiyo spoke in a gentle voice. "May it light your way well, sister. Take care."

"Take care, woman of the snow? It is too late for me to take care. They said my gossiping and whispering caused the trouble. They said my long tongue was to blame. I was never forgiven. I, Kamogawa, who loved the boy." Her voice hardened, a jackhammer now, loud, boring through cement.

"They sent me tonight to bring the talisman. To atone for my wrongdoing. But I will not make your task easy. Let the foreigner choose which is the talisman, if she is able. It was she who caused my misery. I wanted her to pay, but I see my prayers were useless, for she is here. My sorrow will never end."

She closed her right fist and bowed her head. The lantern swayed in her left hand, glowing brightly. The city clock struck the half hour. The woman's fist shot open and three objects fountained from it, falling onto the snow. In the dark I couldn't see what they were, and anyway, I couldn't look down. I was mesmerized – she had me pinned by the eyes like a rabbit in a spotlight. With an effort I forced my eyelids closed, shutting her out. I felt the air grow a little warmer, heard a truck grind along the Saigawa Road and on into the night. Opened one eye just a crack. Then the other. She was gone. Miki was blinking at me in the neon glare and Aunt was hunkered down looking at what the woman had left behind.

There were three paper animals on the snow. Not origami, not folded, but woven with strands of paper thread. *Mizuhiki.* A red dragon. A silver horse. A golden bird.

"Don't touch them," said Aunt Yukiyo. "If we choose badly the first time, there'll be no second chance."

Miki was certain. "It has to be the dragon. It's the only animal mentioned in the message."

Something was caught in the back of my mind, something that made me think I knew what the choice should be. When it came, it was like an explosion in my brain. "It's the bird. We have to choose the bird."

Without hesitation, and before either of them could stop me, I reached down and took the golden bird between my fingers.

Chapter Fourteen

"I have news," said Miki, shaking off her house slippers in the living room doorway. "Big Important Spectacular News."

Okaasan stuck her curly head around the kitchen door. She was roasting soy beans and their hot, nutty smell filled the house. "You're home early, Miki *chan*. It's only just four o'clock. What's your news?"

"School," said Miki dramatically. "It's CLOSED. The influenza is officially an epidemic and the junior high is closed till next WEDNESDAY. Isn't it WONDERFUL?"

Miki hated sitting in school all day. She wanted to be outside, or reading, or doing something she thought was really important, like playing basketball or saving the environment. But I guessed she was especially pleased to have a holiday just now. It would give us the time we needed to decipher the message.

Her father looked up from the table. He was playing *shōgi*, Japanese chess, with Granny. Losing. "Good," he said. "Plenty of time for you to help me in the shop."

"Otooosaan." Miki's face was at its most pathetic.

Otōsan grinned. "The Old Corner needs dusting, the books need sorting, and that centipede kite has a few holes to be mended."

"Or," said Miki, "I could teach Hannah to play the flower card game and take her shopping and sightseeing. And maybe you could take us to the mountains for a day's skiing, Dad."

"Hmmph," said Otōsan. "Then we'll all have the influenza."

It was Otōsan's day off. All the shops in Kabuto Machi closed every Thursday. I'd pulled myself out of a white, foggy sleep at midday to find the world so quiet I thought it might have stopped while I was sleeping. Aunt Yukiyo had left a note to say she'd gone out and we'd talk later. When I wandered back to the Mulberry Tree, Otōsan had just crawled out of bed and Okaasan was making noodles in the kitchen.

Miki came into the room, pulling her hair loose from its elastic and shaking off the snow. Unbound, it reached past her waist. "I walked home with Hiro, Mum. He said you invited him and his grandpa in for the bean throwing. He was really pleased."

"Poor Hiro," said Okaasan. "He doesn't have much to be pleased about these days. I'm glad they're coming. We'd better start getting organized. You girls can do the sweeping and vacuuming. I'll finish the beans and then I'll start dinner."

"Have you got the talisman?" whispered Miki as she

100

rattled around in the broom cupboard.

I nodded and reached into my pocket. The bird sat lightly in the palm of my hand. Its body was a dense shell of interwoven gold. Fine strands of stiff paper, layered and curved, formed its wing and tail feathers. I remembered it lying shiny on the snow. As soon as I'd picked it up, the horse and the dragon had melted into smoky puddles on the snowy ground. My stomach churned just thinking about it.

Miki reached out and took the bird in both hands. "It's so light. Wasn't last night exciting, Hannah? Wasn't it amazing?"

Exciting and amazing? More like frightening and terrifying! "But you were scared, Miki," I said. "I know you were. I could feel it."

Miki nodded. "I was terrified. But it was still exciting and amazing."

"Miki, that doll had red hair. My hair. Didn't you see? And that woman said I took away her life. What did she mean?"

"What she said was weird. She must have thought you were someone else. Or she was crazy. How did you know to take the bird?"

"The cards. I was mucking around in my room yesterday afternoon and the same card kept falling out of the pack. The one with the green and gold bird on it."

"Truly? That's so clever, Hannah."

I wasn't sure if she meant I was clever to have recognized the talisman, or Kai was clever to have shown me how. I decided not to ask.

Miki dragged a broom out of the cupboard and stuck it in my hand. "I saw Aunt Yukiyo up near the markets on my way home from school. And GUESS who she was with? KimiShimi's found her! You sweep out the bathroom and toilet. I'll start vacuuming upstairs."

"KimiShimi's found her? Tell me some more. And why am I sweeping?"

Miki looped the vacuum cleaner hose around her neck. "I'll tell you about Aunt later. Not that there's much to tell. They were just walking along looking very serious. And we're cleaning because we eat the beans off the floors."

"You eat beans off the toilet floor?"

"No, silly. The other floors. But we clean the toilet anyway."

"Miki, what is this bean throwing? Nobody's told me."

"Clean first," called Miki, heading off up the stairs. "Explanation later."

Granny and Otōsan were still playing *shōgi* when I finished my sweeping. Grandpa Honda had joined them and he was slurping beer and giving them advice they didn't want. Miki must have finished upstairs because I could hear the vacuum cleaner buzzing in the shop. Hiro, looking bored and despondent, was on the sofa near the window, scratching Popo behind the ears. I went over and sat beside him. I tried to imagine how it felt, not to live with your parents. My mother was a nut and my father as vague as it was possible to be, but I wouldn't want to lose them. Especially if I didn't know what had happened. Joel was a different matter. Him I could lose and not even notice. Or maybe not, maybe I'd miss him.

I glanced sideways at Hiro and decided to ask him the question no one else wanted to answer. "Hiro, can you explain to me about this bean throwing? I want to know what happens."

Hiro kept stroking Popo's fur and didn't look up, but at least he answered.

"The bean throwing is held on the last day of winter."

I looked out the window. Snow was drifting down. "How can it be the last day of winter? It's still snowing."

Popo climbed into his lap. Hiro tickled him under the chin. "Well, it's the last day of winter by the ancient moon calendar."

Now I was really confused! Was it or wasn't it the last day of winter?

"See, Hannah," said Hiro, "in our time, spring doesn't start till the beginning of March. But the moon calendar is ancient, and in olden times the first day of spring used to be the first day of the new year. *Setsubun* is the ancient New Year's Eve. That makes tomorrow the first day of spring. The night between winter and spring is dangerous – any turning point between seasons is – because demons and spirits are most powerful then. So we have a ceremony to protect us, and it's called 'the bean throwing'."

Miki appeared in the doorway, dragging the vacuum cleaner behind her. "The whole idea of modern *Setsubun*," she interrupted, waving the vacuum cleaner nozzle around so it almost shaved the terrycloth hat off Grandpa Honda's head, "is to bring good things into your home and your family. Not just luck or money, but good health and happiness and harmony as well. So we take beans and we all walk through the house together, saying, '*Oni wa soto. Fuku wa uchi*'."

"So you're telling devils to go outside and luck to come in," I said.

Miki plugged in the vacuum and nodded. "It's just fun, really. And you get to see Dad wearing a mask. He should wear it all the time, it's much better than his face. And you get to throw beans at him."

Otōsan looked up from his game and sighed.

"Why do we throw beans at Otōsan?"

"To make him go outside. He has to pretend to be the *oni*. It's the father's job."

"And what does an *oni* look like? How will I recognize an *oni* if I see one running out the door?"

"They're huge, and red or green, with horns. I don't think you'll see one. When we say *oni* we mean anything bad, like poverty or sickness or failing your exams or losing your job. An earthquake or a fire. Or someone bad. Someone whose heart is wicked."

An idea popped into my head. I didn't want to spend any more nights creeping around shrines being scared out of my mind. Maybe the bean throwing would solve everything. "If this bean throwing gets rid of devils, maybe it will get rid of our ghost."

Hiro sat up as if he'd been shot. "What ghost?" he said. "I haven't heard anything about a ghost. I'm interested in ghosts!"

We had to tell him. He listened quietly and didn't say anything except, "Uh-huh, uh-huh," but I'm sure his spikes got spikier.

"Can I help you solve it?" he asked when we'd finished.

Miki eyed him severely, poked his feet with the vacuum's nozzle. "You can help," she said, "provided we don't have any more nonsense about girls not being brave. Or any rudeness about me not being good at school. We can't all be good at school, you know. Some of us have other talents."

"It's a deal." Hiro grinned from ear to ear. "This is mega-exciting."

It was the first time I'd seen him smile. He looked really nice.

Otōsan's mask was a lurid red, with horns and fangs, a wide grinning mouth, and shaggy hair a bit like his own. He put it on while Hiro and Miki and I raced around the house opening doors and windows. We had to open them so the *oni* could get out and the luck could come in. It made the house cold enough to freeze your arse off, as my dad would say.

We switched on all the lights. Through the open doors and windows we could see snow falling in the dusk. Okaasan handed out the small, greenish-brown beans. Mine were in a tea bowl. Otōsan and Grandpa Honda had theirs in square wooden drinking cups.

"When we've thrown the beans," Okaasan explained, "we pick up the number of beans that's the same as our age and we eat that number. So you and Hiro will eat twelve each, Hannah. Miki'll eat thirteen."

"Will Granny eat eighty-five?"

"That would be too many. No, she'll just eat a few." Okaasan looked up at the sound of feet hurrying down the hall. "There you are, Yukiyo. We were thinking of starting without you."

"Don't do that," called Aunt, hanging up her coat. "I'll put these donuts on a tray and be right with you. Do you have some beans for me?" She was carrying an enormous Honey House takeout box and looking very thoughtful.

We assembled in the shop. Otōsan threw the first handful, his voice booming out from behind the mask. "*Oni wa soto. Fuku wa uchi.*"

"*Oni wa soto. Fuku wa uchi,*" we chorused after him, throwing our beans. They skittered across the shop floor, running into all the corners. Pachi pachi pachi. Ping. They bounced off Otōsan's mask. Into the kitchen, then the living room, toilet and bathroom. Down to the garden entrance. Beans scattering.

"*Oni wa soto. Fuku wa uchi.*"

We hurled handfuls of beans at Otōsan and he shrieked dramatically, ran into the garden in his socks and hid behind the pine tree. Then he came back in and changed into dry socks and we all went upstairs. Miki gave Granny a push up from behind. Beans rolled and pattered down the stairs and some got trodden on. I decided I wasn't eating those.

"*Oni wa soto. Fuku wa uchi.*"

Along the corridor, and into the bedrooms. We stood at the windows and called the incantation into the night. I felt a bit silly, yelling out the window. Hiro stood well back, out of sight of anyone watching from outside, so I think he felt silly too.

When our bowls and cups were empty, Otōsan took off his mask and we scattered through the house to collect our beans for eating. I like to have a system for everything I do. Mrs. Battersby told me it was an annoying character trait and that an obsession with systems makes you a poor team player. But Mrs. Battersby was thousands of kilometers away. So I decided to eat at least one bean from every room in the house except the bathroom and the toilet. I started with one I found under the table in my room – I could be sure no one had trodden on it. Crunch. It tasted like a nut.

I ate five upstairs. Two on the way down. I was in the little porch choosing number eight when I noticed a flicker of movement on the stairs. Only a bean, bouncing. Except … THIS bean was bouncing UP. Not down. Ping. Ping. More beans joined in, bouncing high, popping up the stairs like demented rice cereal. I yelped. Nobody heard. They heard Miki though. She had a foot on the top step, about to come downstairs, and when she saw the bounding beans she shrieked. "YAAAAH!!" Feet came running from all over the house. Aunt sped down the stairs behind Miki, saying, "Ouch," whenever a bean hit her. Grandpa Honda pottered down the hall. Hiro and Okaasan dashed from the direction of the kitchen, propelling a surprised Granny in front of them. We stood gaping.

"It's the wind," said Okaasan firmly, as if daring us to contradict her. "Let's get all these doors and windows closed."

She had barely finished speaking when we heard it. "Oooh." Softly. From behind the shop door. "Oooh. Oooh. OOOOOOH. HELP!!"

We forgot the doors and windows and hurtled into the shop. Otōsan was on top of Granny's blue chair, dancing from foot to foot as if he was standing on a hot plate. "The boy is back," he yelled. "In the Old Corner. See. See. He's got my war fan. He's dancing around with my beautiful war fan. Help. HELP!"

I couldn't see the boy. None of us could. But the war fan was in full flight, jiving up and down and around in circles as if a whirlwind was tossing it.

"Wow," said Hiro.

"Kai?" Miki's voice was a whisper.

SLAM. The door to the street flew open and wind and snow drove in. The fan zoomed across the room and slid into the back pocket of Otōsan's trousers.

"Oooh," said Otōsan.

"Goodness," said Aunt Yukiyo.

"DELIVERY!"

The white van man, that dancer of tangos, stood framed in the doorway, scanning the room. Checking, I guessed, for purple-haired women. His mouth fell open when he saw Otōsan balancing on the blue chair with the rest of us gathered around like boggled chickens.

"Delivery," he said again, staring. "For Maekawa."

He sidled in, eyeing us warily, heaving behind him a tall bundle sheathed in black plastic. Nobody said anything for a minute, but then Okaasan gathered herself together. "Thank you. Put it in the Old Corner, please," she said. "Hiro will help you." She gave Hiro a little push to de-stun him.

Hiro and Delivery Man tugged the bundle across the floor and stood it at the edge of the Old Corner. Then Delivery Man scurried away, leaving the door open. Nobody remembered to ask him where the bundle had come from.

Silence. Hiro reached out a hand to remove the wrap. As he did a grey wind gusted in and spun across the floor to the Old Corner. The centipede flapped against the wall and the masks shuddered. Hiro took a deep breath and pulled at the plastic. Otōsan fell off his chair with a thud.

A suit of samurai armor stood staring at us. A helmet with great gold horns was poised above a black mask. Dark metal gauntlets and thigh pieces, and body armor in black leather.

"Wow," said Hiro again.

Granny started to chuckle. Grandpa Honda rolled some words around his mouth. When he got them out, he told Aunt Yukiyo how beautiful the armor was. Otōsan looked as if he was gong to faint, so Okaasan hauled him towards the kitchen.

"I'm sure you'd like a beer, Otōsan. I've made some dumplings and afterwards we can have the donuts Yukiyo's brought in. You come too, children," she added, glancing uneasily at the war fan, which was still perched in Otōsan's back pocket. "Bring the plastic and put it in the purple bin, please, Miki *chan*."

Otōsan said nothing, but allowed himself to be towed along and deposited at the table in the living room. Grandpa Honda and Granny followed. Hiro and Miki and I trailed Okaasan and Aunt Yukiyo into the kitchen, where Okaasan sat down quite suddenly in a chair.

"Tell me, Yukiyo *san*," she said, "do I need to worry? Are the children in any danger from this ghost?"

Aunt Yukiyo was washing her hands. "Not from this little one," she said. "He's clever – what a hoot when he danced that fan around. But he's just having fun. The only danger is that others not so friendly may follow him, but the bean throwing should keep them under control."

She went to the bench to collect the serving tray on which she'd arranged her donuts. "Just look at that!" she said, and started to laugh. "I rest my case."

Someone had removed the donuts from their tray and lined them up along the kitchen bench. Someone had carefully placed beans on the white tray in the shape of four hiragana symbols. *O. I. SHI. I. OISHII.* Delicious! We stared.

Then Okaasan started to laugh. "I think I agree with you, Yukiyo. What a nice compliment for your donuts. Although I don't suppose the cheeky little pest can eat them!"

"It's really clever, the way he's done that." Miki was gazing at the *OISHII* with admiration.

Hiro was anxious. "Are the donuts still okay?" Miki had told me he was very keen on Honey House donuts.

I studied the four faces around me. They were talking as if Kai was some cute, mischief-making little cousin who'd come to stay. The only people truly perturbed about him were Otōsan and me, and Otōsan was only bothered because he actually SAW the ghost when no one else did. I was bothered that there WAS a ghost.

Okaasan started spooning rice out of the rice cooker and into bowls. "That armor's quite dashing, isn't it? Do you suppose it's got anything to do with our little visitor?"

Aunt pulled a tray of dumplings from the oven. "It's most likely to be another gift for my brother from Professor Kato, don't you think? It may have no connection with Kai at all. Will you carry these to the table, please, Hannah?"

I took the platter from her, wondering if I'd make it to the table without the dumplings flying in circles around my head or tap dancing off the platter. Miki and Hiro followed me, bowls of rice in their hands.

"Aunt Yukiyo's right," said Miki. "There's nothing evil about Kai. We'd feel it if there was."

"A ghost!" Hiro took a deep breath. "How cool is that! Why didn't you tell me before?"

"We thought you might be frightened," answered Miki, grinning. "Don't you both think," she went on, "that if Kai was alive we'd really like him?"

I thought about it. He was young and alone. And like Miki said, there was nothing evil in his presence. Despite his tricks with donuts and mirrors and beans, I was beginning to like him too.

After supper Grandpa Honda stayed on for a game of *shōgi* with Granny, so Miki and I went to let Hiro out through the shop door. We stopped for a moment to look at the armor. The figure was tall and impressively fearsome, glittering gold and black in the orange lantern light.

Miki was the first to notice the smell. She sniffed. "What IS that? It's like incense."

She was right. I sniffed too.

"It's coming," said Hiro, "from that smoke over there."

He pointed. From each horn of the samurai helmet a plume of navy blue smoke fluttered out, barely noticeable in the dark of the Old Corner. We went closer. Hiro reached up to the smoke and ran his hand through it.

"Hooo," said Miki. "Dad won't like this. He won't like this at all."

夂
Chapter Fifteen

arly the next morning I was sitting behind the shop
counter on Granny's blue chair, waiting for Miki to
come downstairs. We had to go to the 7-Eleven to buy bread
for Okaasan, and to the Honey House to pick up Granny's
morning donuts. The day was snowy damp, and thin fingers
of white mist crept through the open shop door. I could see
Otōsan and Grandpa sweeping snow from the footpath with
long straw brooms. Grandpa was looking stylish in a black
tracksuit with white racing stripes, but Otōsan was drooping
like a maudlin willow. I could guess why. The samurai stared
at me from his corner and I stared back. A soft cloud of navy
blue smoke hung around his helmet. Some obscure chemical
reaction must have been taking place inside him, I decided.
Some ancient materials were reacting with pollutants in the

air. Maybe he'd explode.

Swish went the brooms, plop went snow into the gutters. I listened to the soft murmur of the sweepers' voices.

"A fascinating evening, most enjoyable. How are you feeling this morning, Jun?"

"I am a nervous wreck, Grandpa. It is this samurai boy. I am the only one who sees him. My wife says it is nothing to worry about – the boy is just a small ghost, causing no environmental damage. My sister says I am lucky to have such a gift. Now we have a suit of samurai armor that is blowing blue smoke around my shop. Who knows what damage it will do. What will the customers think? What will come next?"

Grandpa Honda's voice was sympathetic. "Perhaps you should take a day off, Jun. Go to a hot spring resort or to the *pachinko* parlor. Or change your diet. Eat more pickled plums to soothe your stomach." Grandpa Honda pondered a moment. "Or try seaweed with vinegared cucumber?"

"I am not bald, Grandpa."

"You soon will be if you keep worrying." Grandpa Honda beat his broom against the gutter to dry it. "How about a strengthening tonic?" He pondered a moment, then turned suddenly towards Otōsan, looking as if he'd just discovered gold. "I have it! *Kumazashi! Kumazashi* fat is loaded with wholesome nutrients. *Kumazashi* will strengthen your nervous system."

Otōsan continued to look gloomy. "My wife is a member of the PRESERVATION OF ALL WILDLIFE SOCIETY.

My daughter belongs to her school's environment club. If they find out I have eaten *kumazashi* I will be in trouble for a month. And I've heard it stinks. Besides – " he glanced furtively over his shoulder and leaned a bit closer to Grandpa " – where would I find it?"

Grandpa hushed his voice. I could only just hear. "Friends tell me *kumazashi* can be found in the vicinity of Mount Hakusan."

I didn't know what *kumazashi* was, but Grandpa certainly had a high opinion of its effectiveness. Maybe it was a medicinal herb like ginseng, although I didn't see why Otōsan eating an herb would make Okaasan angry. And where was Mount Hakusan? I'd have to ask Miki. I could hear her padding down the stairs in her socks and talking to Popo. I buttoned my coat and slipped on my gloves.

The 7-Eleven was up away from the river, in the direction of Omicho Market. I liked walking through the twisting streets and climbing Kabuto Machi's narrow stairs in the mist. Then I remembered there were things I needed to know.

"Miki, what is *kumazashi*?"

"*Kumazashi? Kuma sashimi*. Slices of raw bear meat. Where did you hear that word?"

Raw bear meat. This was unexpected. I speculated as to how a person would go about getting some. Would Otōsan have to catch his own bear? Didn't bears hibernate in the winter?

"I just heard someone say it on the street." I didn't want

to get Otōsan into trouble. Not until I'd thought about it, anyhow.

We bought the bread at the 7-Eleven and backtracked towards the Honey House. Outside the walls of Omicho, Miki took an abrupt hold on my arm and dragged me across the wide street that bordered Kabuto Machi. No waiting for traffic lights for this girl. Luckily there weren't too many cars.

"Hey!"

"Sorry Hannah, but did you want to run into the lovely Kenjiro and friend?"

I glanced back across the street. The older boys from school, the ones who'd laughed at me on my first day, were sauntering along the opposite footpath. Riki, the shorter one, ignored us, but Kenjiro was staring, his face sour and eyes hard.

"WHAT is his problem? What did I do to him?"

"You're different," said Miki. "You're foreign. And you're my friend, and he doesn't like me, never has since primary school. Says I'm snobby. Forget him! Let's go."

Six or seven old men were at the Honey House tables sipping tea. Toshi was wiping down benches and Aunt was heating cinnamon swirls in the microwave. Near the cash register was a vase of red roses with long stems.

"*Ohayō gozaimasu*, Aunt. *Ohayō gozaimasu*, Toshi *kun*."

"Good morning, girls. I have Granny's donuts ready."
Aunt took two cinnamon swirls out of the microwave and popped them on top of the other donuts in the box by her elbow. They smelled delicious. I spotted a Gorgeous

Green Glacier beside a Luscious Lemon. So Granny ate the medicinal donuts too. Maybe that was what made her such a speedy spotter of shoe mistakes.

Miki sniffed at the vase of roses. "Aunt Yukiyo, where did these roses come from?"

"They're beautiful, don't you think? An old friend sent them. Someone I haven't seen in a long time. Now off you go. Granny will be waiting for her donuts."

At the door I hesitated. "Aunt Yukiyo," I said, "where is Mount Hakusan?"

"Hakusan? Southwest of Kanazawa. A marvelous mountain, worshipped as a god. Perhaps we'll go walking there after the snow melts. Where did you hear about it, Hannah?"

"Oh, just on the street. From someone passing by. You know how it is."

As I followed Miki back to the Mulberry Tree I wondered about Mount Hakusan. We had to find the place where the old mountain god waited in the forest. Could the god be somehow connected to this mountain?

Okaasan made us study for most of the day. She said we could have the rest of the school break to sightsee and shop and do whatever we wanted, as long as we got lots of work done that Friday. At four o'clock she wanted to see all of Miki's homework and the history essay she had to write on

"Samurai Customs in the Edo Period." And she was going to test me on fifty *kanji* and check how much correspondence work I'd done. If all that was satisfactory we were free for the rest of the time school was canceled.

At dinner that night Otōsan announced he'd be taking the day off on Sunday. He would be spending the day out in the country and had arranged with Aunt Yukiyo for Toshi to look after the Mulberry Tree.

Okaasan looked surprised. "A day in the country, Otōsan? That will do you good. I have my cooking class this Sunday, but perhaps the children would like to go with you. Which direction were you planning to take?"

Otōsan shot her a shifty look from under his bangs. I thought I could guess why. He was planning a secret Sunday search for *kumazashi*. I could see him straining for an excuse not to take us, but he was too slow.

Miki jumped at the idea of a day out. "I'd love to come with you, Dad," she said. "So would Hannah. And we'll ask Hiro too, if Grandpa Honda doesn't need him in the shop. A day in the country will cheer him up."

Otōsan gave her a sideways grin. I knew he'd have to think of a way to lose us on Sunday. But I thought we should go. I had a hunch we were meant to.

夂

Chapter Sixteen

When I came downstairs on Saturday morning I found the Smoking Samurai parked in a corner of the living room.

"Otōsan says he can't bear having him in the shop any longer," said Okaasan. "I don't mind him really. I think he's rather nice."

"Did you notice his smoke's changed color?" I asked.

"Mmm." Okaasan nodded. "Pretty shade of yellow. Perhaps he has different colors for different days. Or for different rooms. If we ever find out who sent him, we'll ask them. What are you going to do today, Hannah?"

"We thought we'd go and look at the castle gate this morning. And this afternoon Miki and Hiro are going to teach me to play the flower card game."

"That sounds like a good plan," said Okaasan. "Make sure

you wrap up warm. It'll be cold out."

That afternoon I looked at the flower cards spread out
in front of me and went over the scoring again in my head.
Cards with lots of white background and simple pictures were
worth zero. Any card with a *tanzaku* was worth five points.
(Otōsan sold *tanzaku* in the Mulberry Tree. They're long,
narrow pieces of paper used for writing poetry.) Colorful cards
with more complicated pictures earned you ten points. Full
color cards were worth twenty, except for a red and black one,
a picture of a willow branch in the rain, worth zero.

The three of us were gathered around the living room
table, our legs and feet warm from the heat of the *kotatsu*
underneath. We had the house to ourselves. Okaasan was at
the markets, Otōsan and Granny in the Mulberry Tree, and
Aunt Yukiyo was serving in the Honey House, which was
bursting with customers because the day was so cold. Popo
sat on the windowsill washing his face. The black mask of the
armor watched us.

Miki gathered up the cards and began to sort through the
pack. She picked out nine cards and lined them up on the
tablecloth. "You have to remember these, Hannah. They're bonus
cards. Three sets of three. Here's the first set – wild boar with
bush clover, deer with maple leaves, butterflies with peony."

"*Ino ...shika ... cho*," chanted Hiro. "My favorite
pictures."

"What's *ino shika cho*?"

"The cold has frozen your brain, Hannah. *Inoshishi*, wild boar. *Shika*, deer. *Cho cho*, butterfly. *Ino shika cho*."

The second bonus set was cherry, plum and pine, all with red *tanzaku* as a part of their pictures. The third set of bonus cards had *tanzaku* too, with pictures of maple, chrysanthemum and peony.

"The bonus cards are really valuable. The aim of the game is to get the highest number of points, but if you end up with a set of bonus cards and no one else has a set of matching pictures, you win, even though you don't have the most points."

Complicated. I looked at the cards. Worn, rectangular, and each one a little larger than the long side of a matchbox. The backs were black. I wondered if Kai had played this game, and if he'd been clever or lucky.

Miki put the pack down on the table. "Now we each cut the cards to see who gets first go. You start, Hiro."

Hiro cut the pack in half. He turned up a picture of a white crane surrounded by pine trees, its long neck turned to the sun. Twenty points.

"Now you, Hannah."

I turned up the green-gold bush warbler singing on the plum tree. "It's haunting me." I said. "That's creepy."

"Ten points," said Hiro.

Miki turned up a mountain under a full moon. "Twenty points. Hiro and I will have to draw again."

On the second draw Miki got the wild boar in the bush clover, worth ten points. Hiro's card showed a phoenix hovering above violets. It was worth twenty points, so Hiro would take first go.

"But they're not violets," Miki told me. "They're paulownia flowers. Paulownia is a tree about twelve meters tall. Sometimes we call it the empress tree. Its flowers bloom in winter, big clusters of purple flowers. They've got a lovely smell."

As I learned to play I thought about the morning and our sightseeing trip to the castle gate. The white leaden tiles of the fluted roofs had been hidden under a mantle of snow, but I'd seen the windows jutting out from massive stone walls, and imagined boulders being dropped from them. I'd walked where once samurai had ridden into the castle grounds on horses steaming at the nostrils. I'd felt the past alive all around me, just as Okaasan had said. It was easy to imagine the back gate of the castle as it would have been in Kai's time, with retainers striding through the snow in heavy boots, huddled over hand warmers, or smoking tobacco from long red and gold pipes. The warm smell of horse dung and sweat seemed to linger in the winter air. At night there would have been fires lit in round braziers for light and warmth. Kai might have gone to the castle with his samurai father, might have toiled up to the gate through deep snow.

I felt the warmth of the Maekawa living room around me and wriggled my toes against the *kotatsu*. I was glad no one wanted me to toil anywhere in the snow.

Miki won the first game and Hiro the second. I had high hopes of the third. Miki made a pair by putting a ten point iris card on a five point iris card.

"I don't see," she suddenly said, "how Dad's going to go on his great excursion to the country tomorrow. Not in weather like this."

"My grandpa says tomorrow's forecast is for fine weather," said Hiro. "He wanted to go with us but there's no one who can mind the shop. Mum drives on Sundays. I wish she didn't. Anyhow, he says I should go." He took one of the bonus cards, cherry blossom with *tanzaku*, by matching it with one from his hand.

"Of course you have to come, Hiro," I said. "We need you."

He flashed me a shy smile from under his chrysanthemum bangs.

Miki took a scrunchie from her pocket and bundled her long hair into it. "You know how Mum talks about old stories?" she said. "Do you think we're part of Kai's?"

Hiro, deciding on his next move, tapped a finger on his cards. "Isn't everyone part of an old story?" he said.

Miki took another pair. "Like I'm part of Granny's story and she's part of her grandmother's and my grandchildren will be part of mine?"

"Yes," said Hiro. "Like that."

"Aunt Yukiyo said we're the ones who could finish it," I said. "She didn't say we were part of it."

"You mean we're like doctors assisting at an operation?" said Hiro.

"All I mean," I said, "is that if Aunt Yukiyo is right, and if Otōsan's day in the country matches the next part of the puzzle, then we have to go with him."

I didn't mention the *kumazashi*. Miki might tell her mother, and I guessed Okaasan would stop us going if she knew what Otōsan was up to. She might stop us going anyway if the weather didn't improve. I glanced up at the window. Snow was falling as if it would never stop, flakes dropping to earth like white, weightless stones. Outside, it was lying thick on the old pine and the garden wall and making a frosty blanket for a car parked in the lane.

I put down my pair. Two hillside cards. On one card the hillside lay under a full moon. On the other three wild geese flew above it. Thirty points.

"Ha," I said. "I'll beat you two yet."

"No chance." Miki had her head down, concentrating.

"Look at the samurai!"

Miki's head shot up at the alarm in Hiro's voice. So did mine. Red smoke was pouring from the Smoking Samurai's golden helmet, a crimson pall rising towards the living room ceiling.

"Red for danger," I whispered. "I never thought! He's been blowing yellow smoke since this morning. Warning us."

As I spoke, I took my hand away from the cards and the room turned dark and cold. An oppressive mist was pressing against the windowpanes and we couldn't see out. Miki was so startled she dropped her cards. I felt a terrible fear creeping into my heart, the same fear I'd felt that night at the Ninja Temple. We all stared wordlessly at the windows, watching the darkness press closer, a murky wave coming to swallow us up.

"The cards!"

Hiro was sliding away from the table where I'd just put down the two hillside cards. In the room's new darkness they were glowing. Changing color. The grey-green pampas grass covering the hills was turning a shining, shimmering white. The hills were growing taller, broader, into mountains. And on the mountains silvery snow was falling.

The darkness slithered closer, hemming us in. But the silver snow light was growing too. It pushed out from the cards, swallowing the darkness, pressing it back towards the window.

Slowly, slowly, a hundred hammering heartbeats later, the room lightened and grew warmer and the samurai's red smoke turned slowly blue. I heard the others exhale the breath they'd been holding.

Me, I was gasping. "What on earth was that?"

"Something evil." Hiro, big-eyed, spikes electrified. "An *oni*. Something that wanted to frighten us."

"It succeeded," puffed Miki. "I am totally creeped out. Oh NO, what now?"

A plume of blue smoke had detached itself from the samurai's helmet. It loop-the-looped at the tip of Miki's long

126

nose, floated across the room, and through the closed door. We watched it go.

"Should we … ?" whispered Miki.

"Uh huh," answered Hiro. "It's blue. It should be okay. Let's see where it's going."

Blue or not, I made sure I was at the back. We crept across the *tatami* and slid open the door to the little porch. Shut it behind us. No sign of the smoke plume. Everything was quiet. We could hear Otōsan talking to Granny in the Mulberry Tree, but otherwise there wasn't a sound.

Except … a kind of soft pattering. Like small, unseen feet climbing the stairs. And a sniff, like someone trying to stop his nose running. Hiro heard, too. He followed the sounds. Miki followed Hiro. I followed at the back again, just in case.

Upstairs there WAS a sound. We tiptoed along the corridor. It was coming from my room! Not sniffing. Not pattering. It was more like … roaring? Hiro shoved the door open.

The roaring was coming out of the mirror. I was so scared I had to shut both eyes and then open just one for a look. In the mirror I saw the image of a great mountain. Clouds rolled toward it across a smoke-grey sky. A swirling mist, like tulle, swept around its highest peak and a great wall of snow was cannoning down its slopes. We stood transfixed, watching the avalanche in the mirror roll to a slow stop. The roaring ceased. We could hear the wind howling as it whipped dark snow clouds toward the mountain. One of the clouds made the shape of a great white horse.

"That's Mount Hakusan," Miki whispered. "Shirayama, the white mountain. I've never been there but I've seen photographs."

"And look at the cloud on the peak." Hiro's voice was awed. "That must be the horse god. In legend the goddess of Mount Hakusan rides a white horse. I went to her shrine once when I was younger. It was dark and I was little – I don't remember much."

The picture in the mirror faded into swirls of disintegrating mist as we watched, until all we could see were our three goggle-eyed faces. It crossed my mind that if a geisha had owned this mirror, she'd have needed steely nerves.

Hiro was the first to move. He went to the window and leaned against the wall, looking out.

"Maybe the message's 'old mountain god' is the white horse," he said. "Maybe that's the god we're looking for tomorrow. Anyhow, Kai is telling us we're right about Mount Hakusan. We can be sure of that. And of something else. That darkness didn't erupt downstairs by chance. Someone doesn't want us to solve the riddle of the message. We're meant to be frightened. Someone doesn't want us to go."

夂

Chapter Seventeen

On Sunday morning I woke to a white world under a blue sky. Under my bedroom window a crisp wind was shifting the old pine's branches and stirring its ropes, and sunlight was playing shadow games across the snow-blanketed garden.

Otōsan had decided we would take the bus to Nomachi Station and then a local train to a place called Kaga Ichinomiya. He told Granny and Okaasan that he wanted to show us the famous shrine, but I guessed he had information that there was bear *sashimi* in the vicinity. Okaasan said a day out would do us all good, but she glanced at Otōsan now and then as if she suspected he was up to something. Otōsan bolted his breakfast and hustled us out of the house before she could ask too many questions. He was so eager that we got to Nomachi Eki twenty minutes early, and he was in such a good mood he gave us money for hot drinks from the vending machines. I sat on the blue bench in the waiting room and wrapped both hands around my can of Hot Creamy Cocoa. I was looking forward to a day in the country, to the smell of trees and walking in the sun. I was looking forward to the possibility of seeing a bear.

I didn't think killing wild animals was right, and I supposed I should have been shocked that Otōsan had made up his mind to eat bear meat. But the whole idea of eating bear puzzled me, and mostly I felt curious.

We got into the first of the two carriages as soon as the train pulled into the station. A long bench seat covered in crimson plush ran along each wall, and there were luggage racks above our heads and fans strung from the ceilings. The four of us sat down in a row like parrots on a perch. There was a loud buzzing sound like a swarm of angry bees and the train shuddered and squeaked and wobbled away.

We headed south past grey, white and brown houses clustered close to the train line. Yesterday's snow lay thick in their gardens and on roped trees, and clung to black-tiled roofs. The swings of a children's playground were bright in the sun. We'd been traveling for forty-five minutes before forested hills and mountains emerged to the left of the train. I could see dark, smudgy pines and the wispy yellow-green of bamboo. Houses crouched in the hills' shadows, beyond wet rice fields where new shoots poked up through the snow. A farmer in a blue coat stood watching thick black smoke rise from his fire. We chugged past a Buddhist graveyard. In back gardens, women in floral aprons were hanging pink and yellow blankets out to air.

The hills came closer. I could see a road running parallel to the train tracks. It had been cleared of snow, which was piled up along its edges. A moment later the driver announced the terminus. Kaga Ichinomiya.

We followed a trickle of passengers through the station and out the exit, into the road with snow-stacked edges that we'd seen from the train. Shuttered wooden houses backed onto the forest, but there was no one around. The road ran away enticingly to left and right.

Miki looked expectantly both ways. "What now, Dad?"

"Now," said Otōsan, "I have some business to transact along the road to Tsurugi. I want you three to go and visit Shirayama Hime Shrine. It's around here somewhere." He flapped his hands in four or five different directions. "I want you to meet me in two hours' time at a tea house in Tsurugi called the Blue Wisteria. If you have trouble finding it, ask for directions."

"You're deserting us? What kind of business do you do in a tea house, Dad? Aren't you supposed to be looking after us? Does Mum know about this business transaction?" Miki glared suspiciously at her father.

"I am looking after you," said Otōsan. "I'm doing something to further your education. Your mother would approve. And I'm not doing business in the Blue Wisteria, I'm meeting you there. Don't forget, two hours." And he scuttled off down the road in the direction we'd come.

"The cheek," said Miki.

Hiro was looking around. "Shirayama Hime Shrine," he said, "is the shrine dedicated to the goddess of the White Mountain. I told you I'd been there. My parents brought me for the New Year bell ringing." He sighed. "Maybe that was their mistake. People say the goddess gets jealous if lovers visit the shrine together, that she tries to split them up."

Miki unstuck her eyes from Otōsan's disappearing back and flashed Hiro a look that was half sympathy, half impatience. "Don't be silly, Hiro. You're putting two and two together and making seventeen. Now, which way do we go?"

"Give me a minute, bossy boots. I think it's up here."

We followed him a short way up the road, in the opposite direction to the one Otōsan had taken, and then went left up a narrow lane.

"Where is Mount Hakusan?" I couldn't see any mountains at all, let alone the great white mountain we'd seen in the mirror.

"I think you have to go further out along this road to see Hakusan. But the mountain's not what we're looking for. It's a mountain god we need to find, and the place to find a god, or a goddess, is at a shrine. But first we have to find the shrine. Hah, I was right. There's the gateway up ahead."

The stone *torii* was very old. We passed under it into the shrine's grove and on to a long flight of steps covered with snow. Except for the rippling and falling of water there was no sound. The steps climbed up through a forest of towering cedars, their enormous scaly trunks red in the sun. Vines were tangled high in the foliage. One of the cedars, a giant three or four meters in girth, had a straw rope decorated with white paper banners tied around its trunk. We climbed up and up until we came to a second flight of steps, watched over by ancient stone guardian lions. Far below to the right I could see a bright blue bridge spanning a wintry green river. I felt like I was climbing out of the world and into a new, serene place where being square-faced and not knowing thousands of *kanji* wouldn't matter at all. I was safe here.

The stairs ended, and we stepped under a white *torii* and into the wide sunlit space of the shrine. The cedars fluttered leaves fresh green in the sun and soft birdcalls filled the air. The shrine building was long, made of dark wood embellished with gold. A muted drumming came from somewhere inside. We walked across and stood in front of it.

Miki and Hiro put their hands together, bowed and clapped twice. I wondered if I should do the same.

"Why are you doing that?" I whispered.

"To make sure the goddess is listening to us when we talk with her."

"What are you telling the goddess?"

"Shut up, Hannah. We can't concentrate."

I would have liked to talk to the goddess too, but I wasn't sure what to say, so I just stood there feeling peaceful and floaty. All around me, the leaves sparkled shiny wet in the morning sun. The snow on the shrine roof made sucking sounds as it melted, falling chunks splitting and hissing as they hit the ground. A few icy drops spattered my face.

I turned around to look behind me, back the way we'd come. "Hey!!"

"Shhhh."

"HEY!"

"Hannah, shut up! What *is* the matter?"

I pointed. In an enclosure beside the shrine gate was a statue of a white horse, a sturdy war horse about three meters tall. We must have walked right past it on the way in.

"*Atta!*" said Miki.

"*Are da!*" said Hiro. We hurried across the enclosure to look.

Wild yellow eyes stared at us from under a long armored plate that hid half the horse's face. Its bridle was red, with a gold bit in its mouth. Around its neck hung a red rope, and attached to that was a heavy green and blue bell from which strands of small gold bells were suspended. More bells hung from five prongs attached to the back of its red and black saddle. The stirrups were gold and its tail was braided with gold and green.

Miki read the plaque aloud. "It says a priest named Taicho was the first person to climb Mount Hakusan. That was twelve hundred years ago. On the summit he met the mountain goddess riding a white horse. The goddess granted

Taicho enlightenment, so he built this shrine in her honor. Shirayama and Hakusan. Same *kanji*. Different readings. This has to be the place in the message. We're in the forest and this horse is an old mountain god. Do you have the talisman, Hannah? You better do something quickly."

"Of course I have it. But I don't know what to do!"

I reached into my coat pocket and closed my hand around the little bird. It felt warm and light in my fingers. "Should I leave it here?"

Miki had a bright suggestion! Not! "Shouldn't we put it around the horse god's neck or something?"

"How am I going to get it around its neck? The horse is inside his enclosure and I'm NOT breaking in."

I could see the newspaper headlines: HORTICULTURALIST'S DAUGHTER VANDALIZES SHRINE. MOTHER SAYS HYSTERIA A LONG-TERM PROBLEM. If Miki wanted to hang things on this horse she could do it herself.

We stared at the statue in silence and the war horse stared back, glassy-eyed, while all around us the leaves whispered.

"Could I see?"

The childish voice spoke so suddenly that we all jumped as high as if the horse god had said boo.

When we'd recovered, we found a small boy behind us, a chubby munchkin about eight years old. He gazed up at us with black almond eyes so clear they were almost transparent. Otherwise he was ordinary, small-boy-smudgy, dressed in sweatshirt, jeans and sneakers.

"I like birds," said the munchkin, holding out brown hands and grinning so that his eyes twinkled. "That's a bush warbler, isn't it?"

I hesitated, not knowing what I should do. The bird was our talisman, and really important to us in solving the riddle of Kai. I knew it wasn't right just to hand it over to anyone who asked for it. But I gave it to the little boy. I put the golden bird into his cupped palms like I was hypnotized, even though I saw the worried looks on the others' faces. And it was okay. I sort of knew it would be. Watching, I thought the bird settled into the boy's hands as if it was bedding down into a nest. I imagined it fluffing golden feathers, lifting its wings, soaring up through the cedars towards the sky.

"If you want to leave the warbler here," the boy was saying, "I can show you my secret hiding place. He'll like it there."

We looked at each other.

"If no one's got any better ideas," said Miki, "we may as well go and see."

The boy led us back down the steps, past the lion guardians, past the place where I'd looked down on the blue bridge, until we came to the giant cedar hung with rope and white paper streamers. Looking up, I couldn't see its highest branches. If all four of us had tried to join hands around the tree I don't think we'd have succeeded.

"You could live in there," said Miki.

"The *iguisu* can," said the boy. "I'll show you."

I almost asked if he'd noticed this wasn't a real bird, but what the heck! He was only little, Year Three size, and sometimes kids that age aren't much in touch with reality. Besides, for just a minute, when I'd seen the munchkin holding the warbler, I'd thought it might be real too.

He led us away from the steps, moving carefully so as not to damage the undergrowth, and around to the back of the tree. There was a long split in the trunk, and inside the split a section of bark jutted out to form a natural shelf.

"Your *iguisu* has come to the forest early, but he can wait here until the plum blossom blooms and it's time for him to sing. He'll be safe. The old god will take care of him."

"What did you say?" All our heads spun towards him at once, like we'd been choreographed. "The old god?"

"Yes," said the boy. "He's lived always in our forest." His chubby hand reached out to touch the cedar's bark.

"Rope and white paper," murmured Hiro. "*Shimenawa.* This is a sacred tree, a god's dwelling. The place where the old mountain god waits in the forest."

We'd found it! In the end we'd come to the right place. The mirror had been a truthful guide.

"Thanks, um," I began.

"What's your name?" asked Miki.

"Taki," said the munchkin. "My name is Taki."

We left the *iguisu* in his new home and went on down the stairs with our new friend. He was a good talker. He asked our names, how old we were, if we liked school, if we liked soccer, if we liked the shrine, if I liked Japan, where we were going and why. Then …

"Want to see my uncle's frogs?"

"That's really nice of you, Taki, but …"

"We don't have too much time."

"Yes," said Hiro. "I'm interested in frogs."

Miki and I looked at each other. Honestly! Was there something Hiro WASN'T interested in? As if we had the time to look at frogs! Anyway, who wanted to look at FROGS!?

Back in the lane at the bottom of the steps, Taki led us towards a curious house set well back into the forest on our right. Bamboo crowded close all around it, like a protective wall. We plodded after him down the side of the house, pushing between the bamboo on one side and a thick hedge on the other, and came out into a grassy backyard that sloped gently down to a slow, clear stream. Near the house was a long wooden work bench, beside which rows of wooden shelves were stacked with buckets and jars and gardening tools, bundles of twigs, bottles of mysterious green and yellow liquids, and bunches of dried wildflowers. The vegetable plot lay fallow, snow lining its furrows.

We crossed the stream on a bridge of stepping stones, and climbed beside it along a path into the forest. Deeper in the trees, the waters widened into a pond set among reeds and long grasses and mossy rocks. It was warm there – the clearing captured the sunlight and tall trees shut out the wind. We heard the voices before we saw the singers. Frog voices, filling the air with slow winter songs, songs of warmth under mud, and frozen nights, and the first green smells of spring.

The frogs were astonishing. Yellow, emerald, mint-green, sage-green, smooth-skinned or bumpy, clinging to the grasses, peering from the reeds, sunning themselves on the rocks. We watched in wondering silence, until Taki sneezed. The pond waters plopped and rippled, and the singers vanished, except for one old, warty toad who stayed planted on his rock and watched us with bold, bulbous eyes.

"Sorry," said Taki, grinning, not sorry at all.

"Did I see a Firebelly?" whispered Hiro excitedly. "No, no, it couldn't have been, impossible, too warm for them here. Do you have a Firebelly, Taki?"

Taki tipped his head to one side. "Hmmmm," he said. "I'm not sure what they're called."

Miki was staring at the water, confused. "Frogs belong to the summer. And the evening. Why are so many here now, Taki?"

"They're here all year. Frogs are kind of my uncle's job. He's called the Frog Fetcher. Nobody knows how the frogs first came here, but lots of them are very old. And wise, my uncle says. He's pretty wise himself. Today he's away in the forest, but people come here sometimes to talk with him, ask his advice. Or just to sit by the pond and think. There's been a Frog Fetcher in this place almost since the shrine was built."

"An old place for old stories," said a sweet-sounding voice from the trees.

Taki looked up and grinned. "Hello, Auntie Frog Fetcher. This is Hiro. And Miki and Hannah."

"Welcome, Hiro and Miki and Hannah," she said, gliding into the clearing. She wasn't your average auntie-type. For a start her hair was short and shaggy and a startling pea green. I suddenly felt enormously pleased that other people besides me had relatives who dyed their hair embarrassing colors. But Auntie Frog Fetcher did have a kind of hippy-punk chic. She was wearing a dress in soft, floaty, yellow-greens and browns, like trees put through a blender. And yellow rain boots.

"You came here today to see the shrine?"

"They came to bring a bush warbler. A paper one. We left it in the old god's tree. They said it was a talisman."

Auntie Frog Fetcher looked at us more closely. I had the uncomfortable feeling she was looking inside my head. "A talisman? Does your talisman belong to an old story? Has it brought you luck?"

That was a funny question! None of us really knew what to say, but Auntie Frog Fetcher obviously expected an answer.

Finally Miki spoke up. "The talisman does belong to an old story," she said hesitantly, "but it isn't ours. We brought it here for someone else. Sort of as a … favor."

Taki's auntie looked at us again in her weird, green, slightly uncomfortable way. "Yes," she said. "I understand. And one good turn deserves another. Come with me. There's something I want you to have. Let's call it a souvenir of your visit to Kaga Ichinomiya."

We trooped behind her down the path to the house. The auntie went directly to the wooden shelves and selected a glass jar with a screw top lid. It seemed to be full of twigs and leaves and bits of grass. She handed it to Miki.

"Mugwort, shepherd's purse, cutweed, chickweed, bee nettle, turnip, daikon radish greens," she said. "The seven herbs of spring, and some medicinal grasses from the Hakusan foothills. There's a saying in the Frog Fetcher family that this mixture is so powerful it can warm cold stone and make dragons happy. Keep it safe, keep it with you. The time of the deep snow is coming and you may find it useful."

The hair at the back of my neck prickled when she said that. It was almost like she knew, or guessed, that something strange was happening to us.

Miki was peering at the jar. "Thank you, Mrs. Frog Fetcher. These look just like the herbs my Aunt Yukiyo uses to make her Gorgeous Green Glaciers."

"If your aunt understands such herbs, she is indeed a wise woman. But what is a Gorgeous Green Glacier?"

"A kind of donut."

"I think you'll find it's much more than a donut. Go safely now, children. I must go back to my trees." And with a swish of her foresty skirts she was gone.

Miki gave Hiro the jar, and he put it carefully in his parka pocket and closed the zipper.

"So now I think we have the gift," he murmured.

"Solving Kai's riddle is kind of like doing a jigsaw puzzle.

The pieces slot themselves in place, and you don't have any idea what the final picture should look like until you've finished it."

We said goodbye to Taki, turned away from that green place, with its wisdom of old frogs and warm ponds, and set off towards the Tsurugi road. From somewhere deep in the forest came the liquid notes of a bird song. I wondered if it could be our bush warbler calling goodbye.

文

Chapter Eighteen

Fields stretched away to our left and tree-covered hills climbed steeply to the right. The sun was warm, but a cold wind and a buildup of clouds promised rain or snow later in the day. The walk took us thirty minutes. Tsurugi was the largest town near Mount Hakusan and famous for *sake*, walnuts, knives and drums. I knew because Granny had insisted on telling me. Now I had the shoe thing down, she'd taken over as Education Minister.

We asked directions for the Blue Wisteria from an old man sitting in the sun by the roadside. It turned out to be a *sushi* restaurant. We peered through the door at wooden stools lined up at a kind of breakfast bar. There was no sign of Otōsan and no other customers, so we hung around outside for fifteen minutes, sitting on a wooden bench and wondering what we would do if he didn't show. We were just deciding to go in and ask the staff if anyone had seen him when a pointed nose attached to a tall, thin man in a chef's outfit came out the door. A wide green sweatband held his blond hair off his forehead.

As soon as he spotted us he beetled up to me and spoke in English. "Would you be speaking English?" he asked.

"I would be," I answered.

"And would you be being the persons accompanying the *kumazashi* eater?"

"We … er … might be," I said.

"What did he say?" asked Hiro.

I translated.

"What does he mean, 'the *kumazashi* eater'?" asked Hiro. "What *kumazashi* eater?"

"*Kumazashi*? Oh no!" Miki clapped both hands to her mouth. "It's Dad, isn't it? What's he done?"

I turned back to Green Sweatband. "We are," I said, "the persons accompanying the *kumazashi* eater."

The tall blond one looked relieved. "The *kumazashi* eater is been haffing a small accident. He is been haffing trouble getting rid of a lady. I am haffing trouble getting rid of him. And of her. They are both being in my kitchen, I do not want them. Please accompany."

I translated.

Miki gasped. "A lady? What lady? What's he doing with a lady?"

The chef led us through the restaurant and into the

144

kitchen. Otōsan was flopped on a chair in one corner.
He looked green and very guilty, and he smelled funny.
Beside him stood a woman carrying a folder. As we came
in she turned and glared at us as if we were spiders she was
considering stepping on. If Otōsan was having a romantic
fling, it obviously wasn't going well. We seemed to have
interrupted the lady mid-tirade.

"Good afternoon. You ought to be ashamed of yourselves,"
she said.

We goggled.

"I am Keiko Higuchi, the president of the Tsurugi Society
Against the Consumption of Bears and Badgers." She opened
the folder and brought out three pamphlets with large black
bears on the covers. She handed one to each of us.

"Please read your pamphlets carefully and change your
ways. Bears are beautiful animals. They are not for eating.
They are for looking. It is cruel to kill them, either with guns
or with poison arrows, as in the past. Their raw meat is tough,
and it stinks and is very unpleasant for others to smell on your
breath. I am sure you can smell this one here."

She gestured towards Otōsan who slumped further down
in his chair.

"And if, like this one here," she gestured again in Otōsan's
direction, "if you eat the flesh of a bear that does not live in
the heart of the mountains, but lives near homes or villages
and eats human garbage, you will suffer food poisoning. That
might teach you a very good lesson, as I am hoping it has

taught this one here. He was lucky I found him when he had eaten only one small mouthful."

If Otōsan felt lucky, he wasn't letting on.

Miki was staring at him in horror. "Dad, you haven't been eating … You couldn't! … I can't believe! … Mum's going to be furious!"

"He has," said Folder firmly, "been eating *kumazashi*."

Miki turned to me. Suspicious. "Hannah, what do you know about this? Why did you ask me what *kumazashi* was the other day?"

"I … um …"

I was saved because the cook, who looked as if he was tired of being ignored in his own kitchen, coughed.

Folder turned her attention towards him. "And you," she said, "coming from Iceland or Greenland or wherever it is and polluting our town by serving raw bear meat … you also should be –"

"I am not speaking Japanese," said the cook.

I translated for him and he bristled up like a Blue Tongue into a long thin streak of indignation.

"Please be telling her," he said to me, "that I am from Denmark. My name is Valdimar and I am not serving any *kumazashi* in this restaurant. That one there purchased it from a person of disreputable reputation whose name I am knowing but not telling. It is not my fault if he sits on the bench outside my restaurant when he is feeling woozy. I am coming to Japan to learn to make *sushi* only. Now I am finding *kumazashi* eaters and obstropolous womens in my kitchen. My friend and I wanted to go skiings this afternoon, but I must cancel. I cannot go and be leaving peoples fighting in my kitchen."

Poor Valdimar.

"I'm sure," I said, as politely as I knew how, "that my friend's father didn't mean to cause you trouble. Do you think he could have a cup of tea? Just to settle his stomach?"

By the time Valdimar had persuaded the anti-bear-consumption lady to leave (when begging and pleading failed, he sang Danish folk songs at the top of his voice, which did shoo her away but was terrible for the rest of us), and Otōsan had finished his tea, rain was drizzling down the Blue Wisteria's windows. Valdimar bent his long body to look out.

"You will be getting very wet," he remarked, "on the way to the station." He sounded very pleased.

Miki and I scrabbled around in our backpacks for our umbrellas and Hiro opened his big, tartan umbrella, which he'd been carrying over his shoulder all day. Miki's umbrella was black. Mine was covered in tropical flowers (I'd brought it from home). Otōsan, a bit livelier after the tea, hobbled to get his from the Blue Wisteria's umbrella stand. It was the same tomato red as a station master's flag.

The walk to the station took longer than we'd expected. Traffic whizzed by us while a slow drizzle pattered down on our umbrella skins. My legs were cold and tired and aching.

Beside me, Miki was still fuming, glaring balefully at

147

Otōsan's back as he ambled along in front of us.

"Someone, Hannah," she said in her loudest voice, "it might have been Aunt Yukiyo, told me that ghosts get dreadfully angry if they hear of people eating wild animals. Ghosts are very fussy about the environment."

I heard Otōsan gulp out a small, "Ooh."

"Did you say something, Dad?" Miki called to him.

Otōsan cleared his throat. "Um … ah … wouldn't ghosts understand if a person ate a wild animal for medicinal purposes?"

"Absolutely not," Miki assured him. "Ghosts don't understand medicinal purposes."

Otōsan pottered on, looking positively funereal. A little way ahead plodded Hiro, head tilted thoughtfully. He seemed to be enjoying himself.

"You know, Hannah," he said as we boarded the train, "I've been thinking. I've been thinking that the appearance of this ghost has something to do with you."

"Me?" I stared at Hiro as if he'd gone crazy. I decided he probably had. "What could Kai possibly have to do with me? I just arrived in Japan!"

"He arrived the day you did," said Hiro. "The flower cards were pulled out of your hands. Your mother slid down the stairs for no reason. The pictures are appearing in your mirror. He threw the donuts at you. The *shakuhachi* player gave you the sleeve lantern, and the straw doll at Sarumaru Shrine had red hair. It's got to be more than coincidence. You could be linked to Kai's story. What do you think, Miki?"

But Miki was busy thinking her own thoughts. Otōsan had nodded off to sleep in his seat. He looked decidedly damp.

夂

Chapter Nineteen

That night after dinner I went to Miki's room and collected Kai's toy box. Back in my own room I took the lid off and spread his toys on the floor. The whirligig, the wooden sailboat, the black and white shells of the *Go* game. The square sheet of paper with the written message. And a few odds and ends: a broken hairpin, a scrap of yellow silk, and two buttons, one brass and one made of blue glass. Was Hiro right? Were Kai and I connected somehow? I couldn't think of any way it might be possible.

I picked up the blue glass button. Traditional Japanese clothes don't have buttons, and I wondered where Kai might have gotten it. It was daisy-shaped, and underneath the bits of dust and grime caught in the creases between the petals it was the color of a summer sky. I spat on it and rubbed it with the tail of my shirt. Better. I was holding it up to the light and watching it sparkle when Miki put her head around the door. She took in the toys spread on the floor and then her eyes went to the button.

"Is it from Kai's box?" She took it from me and held it to the light like I'd done. "It's the same blue as your eyes, Hannah. Why don't you put it on your charm bracelet? We could attach it with a bit of wire."

"Where would Kai have found a button like that, Miki? It's not Japanese, is it? It looks European."

"Maybe it wasn't his," said Miki. "Maybe someone put it into the box years later. You know how people dump things in boxes when they can't think what else to do with them."

I held the button in the palm of my hand and folded my fingers around it. "I think I will keep it," I said, "if you think it's okay. What did you decide about the *kumazashi* excursion? Did you tell Okaasan?"

I'd been on tenterhooks all through dinner, wondering if Miki was going to spill the beans. She shook her head.

"I couldn't. Dad looks so miserable. Not that I'm not really mad at him over it. He knows how strongly Mum and I feel about protecting our wild creatures." She gave a wicked grin. "Anyway, I thought it might be useful to have a bargaining point with Dad. We might get that day's skiing out of him yet."

After she'd gone I put everything back in the box, slipped the lid on and slid under my quilt. I switched off the reading lamp and looked up to the night sky framed in the window.

More snow was forecast. The time of the deep snow is coming, Auntie Frog Fetcher had said. As I fell into a long tunnel of dreamless sleep I wondered where frogs went in bad weather.

When I woke the next morning I thought I'd been running up and down a staircase, laughing. I looked up at the window and saw snow pouring from the sky.

"Birds," said Okaasan crossly, plonking down her shovel and dusting snow off her clothes as she came in from the garden. "Birds have eaten every one of my cabbages. There's no food for them in the mountains this winter, and with this heavy snow, things will only get worse."

I peered out the door. The garden was an iced cake, blanketed in white. Icicles clung to the old pine's ropes. The cabbages Okaasan was talking about weren't cabbages for eating, at least not by people. They were decorative cabbages. She grew them in pots lined up against the wall. They looked like big, lumpy, purple and white flowers, but Okaasan was very proud of them.

"And where did this come from?" Okaasan had pulled a red paper umbrella out of the umbrella stand and was holding it up by its bamboo handle. A faint smell of lacquer and oil emanated from it.

"Don't know," said Miki. "Unless … didn't Dad have a red umbrella with him yesterday?"

Okaasan tsked. "First he goes off eating *kumazashi*," she

said. "Then he can't even bring home my brand new umbrella. I suppose he's picked this one up by mistake. Just look at the state of it. It's positively dilapidated."

She opened the umbrella and we saw there was a tear in one of the triangular paper strips between its ribs.

"So you know about the *kumazashi*, Mum! Who told you?"

"Otōsan did," said Okaasan. "I was very cross until I realized he only did it because he's so worried about this boy, Kai. It would be much better for us all if he didn't see ghosts. He finds it very stressful."

"A torn umbrella hides a soul among its ribs," crackled Granny, pattering in through the garden door and stamping her long rubber boots. She'd been sweeping the edges of the garden path as Okaasan shoveled away the snow.

"Granny," said Okaasan, "today I don't want to hear one word about souls or ghosts or small samurai boys. Not one more word. It's bad enough that the great suit of armor in the living room has been blowing out yellow smoke for the past hour. I don't mean I don't like the samurai, because I do. But why does his smoke have to smell? I'm not saying it's not a good smell, it's a little like freshly cut timber. I'm just saying that if he must blow smoke around, I'd prefer it was odorless. Every time Otōsan smells it, he shudders and shivers. I'm very worried about him."

Miki and I looked at each other. Yellow smoke! A warning.

"We better go see Aunt Yukiyo," Miki said.

As soon as we could, we collected Hiro and headed for the Honey House. Aunt found us a corner table and came to sit down too, bringing hot chocolate and a stack of donuts. There was a Gorgeous Green Glacier for each of us, as well as Grinning Gingers and Honey Happinesses. Aunt was very interested to hear about the Frog Fetchers.

"I've heard of that family," she said. "They're devoted to their frogs, and it's said the one they call Auntie is a marvelous herbalist."

"She gave us a jar filled with herbs and grasses. She said they'll warm cold stone and make dragons happy."

Aunt Yukiyo raised her eyebrows. "That's a precious gift. I hope you're taking good care of it. Where are the herbs now?"

"In my room," said Miki. "On the bookshelf. That's where I left them."

"A gift like that isn't to be taken lightly, Mikiko. It shouldn't be left lying around."

Hiro's face blossomed with apprehension. "Didn't you say the samurai's blowing yellow smoke? We'd better go and check on those herbs!"

The jar was gone.

"Of course it is," said Okaasan crossly. "Someone came to the door collecting jars and bottles. For winter pickles, I

154

think. I saw that jar of weeds in your room earlier, Mikiko. If you wanted to keep it, you should have put it somewhere safe. You know I'm a recycler."

"Who was it? Who was collecting? Which way did he go?"

"Towards the river, I think. And it was a boy from your school, a big boy, a Third Year, Kenjiro someone."

"Not Kenjiro Kamogawa? That dirty sneaking piece of slime! That sly excuse for a human being! Mum, how could you?"

"Kamogawa?" The name rang a bell. "Wasn't that what the woman at Sarumaru Shrine called herself?"

Miki nodded. "Kenjiro is probably a descendant. He's every bit as gruesome."

"Stop talking and let's go," said Hiro. "We've got to catch him."

We grabbed our scarves and coats and umbrellas, shoved our feet into boots, and hurtled like maniacs down the hill towards the river, slipping and sliding on crusty patches of ice. At the river we stood puffing, backs against the stone rampart, peering through the snow curtain to the right and left. A line of tea and coffee houses ran along the river street. Snow blanketed their roofs and lay piled across doorways. The Asano ran winter wild. Deep grey and swollen, water pounded and foamed across its rocks. The river banks were thick with powder snow, the willows frozen sculptures. My face hurt with the cold and my mouth had gone numb and I couldn't speak. No sign of movement and no sound. We'd lost him.

"Look. Over there. Is that who we're looking for?"

Hiro's eyes were sharp. About thirty meters to our left, someone had taken shelter under the eaves of a tea house. I could barely see his outline through the blinding snow.

"Let's go very quietly," whispered Miki. "We'll keep as close as we can to the houses and creep along and surprise him. But even if we corner him, it'll be a miracle if we can persuade him to give us back our jar. He's really mean. Put your umbrella down, Hannah. It's too bright – he'll see us coming."

When we were a couple of meters from the boy, Miki called out. "Kamogawa *kun*. You have a jar that belongs to us. I would like to have it back, please. My mother gave it to you by accident."

Kenjiro Kamogawa started, then turned to face us. Big and nasty. He had hold of a burlap bag that made a clinking noise as he moved.

"Get out of here, Maekawa," he growled. "Who do you think you're dealing with? I saw all those weeds in your crappy little jar. Reckon I'll chuck them in the trash can as soon as I get home. You got a problem with that?"

"I'm asking politely, Kamogawa *san*."

"I don't give a rat's about politely, Maekawa. You can take yourself and your pathetic primary school friend and Shorty from Australia and get out of here."

I felt rather than saw Hiro tense up. Me, I got mad. I could feel the anger running up the back of my neck and

156

spurting out my cheeks. I could feel it balling my fists and curling my toes. It was boiling over. I took a run and a flying leap and smacked into the big oaf's chest, pushing him off balance. He dropped his sack with a rattling crash and we thudded together onto the snowy ground.

"Thief!" I heard myself yelling in English. "Rotten mongrel thief. It's our jar and we're taking it back."

I grabbed his ears and pulled them really hard. Joel hates that. Then I tried to wedge his nose between my fingers and twist it, but my gloves were wet and my hands were cold, and Kenjiro's nose was smaller than Joel's, which made it difficult to get a grip. And he was really strong. I decided I was in big trouble!

"WHAT IS THIS COMMOTION?" a deep voice bellowed. "WHAT'S GOING ON? STOP IMMEDIATELY."

I heard Kenjiro gasp, felt his weight lift. Running feet scurried away along the street. I lay flat on the snow for a moment until I'd caught my breath, and then I sat up. A tall man in a wide-sleeved black jacket and the traditional man's skirt, the grey *hakama*, was striding purposefully down the street away from us. He had a *shakuhachi* in his left hand and was brandishing it in the direction of Kenjiro's disappearing back. I guessed he'd come out of the tea house.

"How dare you attack a little girl?" he was yelling. "How dare you? Great lout."

A husky voice, deep and syrupy. Like warm honey. A voice I knew, because I'd heard it once at the Ninja Temple and once, very softly, in the Mulberry Tree.

The man came striding back and bent over me. "Are you all right, little girl?"

I peered up through the snow into the handsome face of KimiShimi. Beside him stood Hiro, clutching the jar of herbs.

The tea house outside which we'd created the rumpus was called the Singing Flute. It wasn't open, but KimiShimi ushered us inside.

"Are you sure it's okay, Shimizu *san*?" asked Miki. "Will the owner mind us coming in?"

"I'm the owner," said KimiShimi, "and I don't mind at all. Sit here by the heater. I'll make you a hot drink."

I watched KimiShimi as he bustled around behind the bar putting cups on a tray. Miki was watching him too.

"His face was in shadow at the temple," I said. "But why didn't I recognize his voice in the Mulberry Tree?"

"Well, he was whispering," she answered. "Besides, who would connect spunky KimiShimi with a monk of … whatever it was?"

"Emptiness and nothingness," supplied Hiro, holding his gloves out to the heater to dry them.

KimiShimi came back with a laden tray. He set it down on one of the tables, poured tea for himself and cocoa for us. On a plate were some tiny cakes. "The same kind my nephew gave you at the Ninja Temple, Hiro. My sister cooks them for me."

Miki took a noisy gulp of her chocolate, eyeing me over the rim of the cup. "You know, Hannah," she said, "Dad's *kumazashi* excursion won't rate a mention when Mum finds out you've been brawling in the street with a Third Year boy."

I groaned. "Don't talk about it, Miki. I can't bear to think what Okaasan will say. And wait until MY mother hears about it! She'll be livid. It's just that I got so angry."

"Stop teasing her, Miki," said Hiro. "No one will hear about it from us, Hannah. And you won't say anything, will you, Shimizu *san*?"

"Not a word," said KimiShimi. "But what about this Kenjiro character?"

"Not likely," said Miki. "He was winded by a First Year girl. He won't talk."

I watched KimiShimi's spectacular face as he sipped his tea. He'd given me the sleeve lantern and started us on our mission to help Kai. Why? He looked up suddenly and smiled, as if reading my thoughts.

"I expect you're curious about the lantern, Hannah. It's a long story, a story that started twelve years ago, when Yukiyo *san* left me and went to live in Aomori."

Miki butted in, eyes popping. For such a polite girl she's a terrible butter-in-er!

"Aunt Yukiyo left you? We always thought that you left her, that she went to Aomori because you broke her heart."

"I did break her heart," said KimiShimi. "And she broke mine. I used to be a very brash young man, ambitious and ruthless, careless of nature and the spiritual world. Yukiyo loved me, but there were traits in my character she couldn't

159

live with. So she went away. I have become a different person in the past ten years. Learning to play the *shakuhachi* changed my life. I took the lantern to the Ninja Temple that night because my instincts told me it might be needed. And there you were, Hannah, a foreign child in a strange land, looking frightened and cold. I thought a gift might help. Losing Yukiyo taught me many things. One of them was kindness."

He smiled his beautiful smile again. "Now, you children should finish your tea and get off home, before Okaasan starts to worry. I'll telephone the Mulberry Tree and let them know you're on your way. I daresay we'll see each other again soon."

夂

Chapter Twenty

We said goodbye to KimiShimi and walked out into the snow. About ten meters along the river alley, Hiro, the jar of herbs safe in his pocket, led the way towards home, down a street so narrow it seemed like a secret passage between the silent houses. The thick, white hush of deep snow pressed in on us. On we went from one narrow lane to another, deeper and deeper into the heart of Kabuto Machi. I felt like a wombat in an endless white tunnel. A nasty little wind was rising, reaching icy fingers along the lanes and scattering cold flurries of snow in our faces. Before long we were struggling through a tossing white haze.

"I never heard wind like this in Kanazawa. I've lost my direction. Do you know this part of Kabuto Machi, Hiro? Should we take shelter?" Miki's voice was muffled.

Hiro shouted back against the wind's moaning. "I thought

I knew where I was going but now I'm not so sure. Everything looks different. Do you know anywhere we could go?"

The wind was whipping the snow and shooting it into our faces like bullets. I shut my eyes to close out the whirling whiteness and bumped into Miki, who'd come to a sudden stop.

"I don't, but here's as good as anywhere. See, the Turtle House. The *noren* are down, so it's open. Must be a tea house or a restaurant. I'm sure they'll let us shelter till the weather calms down."

Hiro slid the door open. Inside, it was very dark. We piled into the entrance hall, calling "*Gomen kudasai.*" Outside the wind howled louder. Hiro called again. "*Gomen kudasai.*" No answer, but slowly a light grew on the wall above us, until we could see the head of a great turtle carved in wood, with light pouring orange from its gaping mouth.

A dusty voice floated towards us out of the shadows. "Three children," it said. "Children caught in the snowstorm. Nothing to worry us, sisters. Welcome, children."

As the light grew, three elderly ladies came into view. They were standing in a doorway above us, dressed in kimonos, purple, green and silver-grey. One wore an enormous pair of horn-rimmed spectacles. One wore silver hoop earrings. The third had a pretty paisley shawl around her shoulders.

"We are the Sugihara sisters," they chorused. "Please come in out of the storm."

"Is this a good idea?" I muttered to the others as we pulled off our boots and hung up our coats. "The house feels a bit odd and so do they."

Hiro shrugged. "We don't have a choice. Just listen to that wind."

He had a point. The wind was roaring, hammering the door behind us with fistfuls of hard snow.

The Sugiharas led us down a pinched passageway into a square *tatami* room where they lined up in a row and introduced themselves formally, saying their surname first.

"Hajimemashite. Sugihara Yawarakai *desu*." Purple kimono, blue *obi*, horn-rimmed spectacles.

"Hajimemashite. Sugihara Amai *desu*." Silver-grey kimono, crimson *obi*, hoop earrings.

"Hajimemashite. Sugihara Suppai *desu*." Deep-green kimono, lemon *obi*, paisley shawl.

Their names were very peculiar. Yawarakai, "Soft." Amai, "Sweet." Suppai, "Sour." Adjectives! As the thought popped into my head, Amai, the one with the hoops, spoke.

"You'll be thinking," she said, "that our names are a little odd. I can't tell you how many people have said so, so we've learned to explain before they make remarks. Our parents named us after the taste or texture of their favorite food for the year each of us was born. Yawarakai was for tofu. Amai for bean jam buns. And Suppai for lemons, which they ate nonstop for not one but two years. The acid took all the enamel off my father's teeth. Now please tell us who you are. We're SO interested in names. The boy first."

Hiro stepped forward. "Honda Hirotaka *desu*."

"A good name for him," remarked Yawarakai to her sisters. "'As high as the sun.' He will be too. Be very famous, I mean."

"Maekawa Mikiko *desu.*"

"'The child of three happinesses'," remarked Amai. "It's true there'll be much happiness for you, Mikiko. A little sadness too. But you'll give much happiness, which is perhaps even more important. Don't you think so, dear?"

"Forrester Hannah *desu.*"

"Was that Hana you said, dear? A flower? I'm not sure how appropriate … but of course." Suppai clapped her hands maniacally for at least five seconds. "It's to do with her becoming a healer. Herbs and medicines. Yes. Yes."

She looked enormously pleased with herself as her sisters clucked agreement.

"Now that we know each other," Suppai went on, "it's time for the poems."

Hiro and I looked at each other.

"I beg your pardon," said Miki. "What poems would those be?"

"*Haiku,*" said Amai. "The *haiku* poems we're all going to write. Monday's poetry day at the Turtle House. To the poetry room!"

And she wheeled out the door like a knight leading her followers into battle. We trailed after her because we didn't know what else to do.

She led the way on to the wide, wooden corridor that ran all around the house. To our left we could see out through a glass wall into the garden, where the snowstorm was tossing and fretting. All along the corridor on our right were sliding paper doors leading into different rooms. Each door was covered with a brightly colored painting.

"Refresh my memory," I whispered as we bundled along after the sisters. "A *haiku* has how many syllables?"

"Seventeen," hissed Miki. "Five in the first and third lines. Seven in the second. Just make one up so we can get out of here. Anything will do. I'm no good at them either."

Hiro was at the back of the group. I heard him mutter, "Wow." Then he grabbed both our arms. I almost tipped over backwards.

"Have you noticed the doors?" he whispered.

"Great raving balls of fire," I said.

My father says that a lot when he's really shocked about something. And I was REALLY shocked! I couldn't believe I hadn't noticed. The paintings on the paper doors were the pictures on the flower cards, the colors saturated, and the scale magnified a hundred times. Over my shoulder I could see the butterfly with peonies. Beyond that was the maple with deer. Beside us were the vibrant colors of cherry blossom. Ahead, Yawarakai was sliding open a door covered in the purple blossoms of the paulownia tree.

"Welcome to our Winter Room, my dears," she cooed.

I met Miki and Hiro's eyes, and saw that they already understood. We were in the House of Cards!

Amai gave everyone a white *tanzaku*, one of the long,

thin papers used for poetry writing, just like the ones pictured on the flower cards. Suppai handed out fine brushes and we all folded our legs under us and sat at the low table, except Yawarakai, who stayed standing. She bowed, and said, "Today we will write about the things we hope for, the things closest to our hearts. Five minutes. Let's begin!"

Five minutes! I gazed desperately around the Winter Room for inspiration. To my right was the crane with the pine trees, for January. To my left the bush warbler and the plum blossom, for February. And the paulownia flowers for December on the door behind. The painting on the door directly in front of me was a simple winter scene, pines under a night sky, and didn't belong to the flower cards. I had to think! What was it I most wanted? What was closest to my heart? Then inspiration came in a flash and I started to scribble in *hiragana*.

When I looked up the others were all still writing. Maybe I was pretty good at *haiku*. I stared straight ahead, feeling tired, thinking of nothing. Bit by bit the painted screen in front of me came into focus. A sliver of moon shone down over a grove of pines powdered white with snow. Beside the trees a road ran into the distance. I'd been staring a few minutes when I noticed a faint light moving through the trees, so pale it was barely there.

"Stop writing."

Yawarakai's voice made me jump. I'd been miles away. The question just popped out before I thought about it. "Did you know there's a light in your picture?"

The three sisters turned as one to stare at the grove of pines.

"No light," said Amai. "I don't see a thing."

"You couldn't be more wrong!" Suppai folded her arms.

"We don't like talk of lights," said Yawarakai.

"The sun plays funny tricks."

"And the moon. We never saw anyone in the grove the night the child escaped. We're sure we didn't."

"Shhh!"

"Oh dear, just look at the time." Suppai scanned the room for a clock. There wasn't one.

"We mustn't hold you up any longer, children, now the wind's gone. But thank you for the beautiful poetry."

"One of us will show you out."

"You'll have to choose which one," said Amai. "Those are the house rules."

"Leaving is not the same as entering." Yawarakai polished her spectacles.

"It should be me," said Suppai. "It's my turn."

"Choose, choose," chorused the sisters.

"Could Yawarakai *san* show us out please?" asked Hiro politely.

"She always gets picked," said grumpy Suppai.

"We don't see why," muttered Amai.

They bowed us sulkily out of the room, and Yawarakai led us to the front door and let us out into a still, white afternoon, blinking kindly through her horn-rims. I was glad to be out of the Turtle House. It was calm now in the streets of Kabuto Machi. People were coming out of their shops and houses, mostly to shovel away the snow.

"That was a weird experience. They didn't even bother listening to our *haiku*. What on earth did you see in the picture, Hannah?" Miki was scrunching her *haiku* paper up into a ball. She threw it in the first rubbish bin we came to.

"You might need that poem," I said. "And I didn't see anything really. It just looked like a light was moving in the trees. It was probably a shadow moving somewhere in the house. I can't see why they were so strange about it."

"Imagine us finding the House of Cards like that. But we don't have the winter words," said Miki.

"Yes we do. The sisters' names. They have to be the words."

"They don't have much to do with winter. And speaking of names, what made you choose Yawarakai to show us out, Hiro?"

"Her *obi*," he answered. "Blue for safety. The sisters were probably harmless but I didn't want to take any chances."

"So," said Miki, "tomorrow we go to the lord's garden, Kenrokuen, at dawn."

"Kenrokuen doesn't open until eight on winter mornings," said Hiro. "How are we going to get around that?"

"Aunt Yukiyo," said Miki. "She'll fix it."

夂

Chapter Twenty-One

We didn't turn on any lights. In the somber, pre-dawn world we crept downstairs and shrugged into our coats.

"Better bring an umbrella," said Miki, "just in case it starts to snow again."

I fumbled for one in the dark and slid into my boots. Hiro was waiting like a silent, sleepy mushroom outside the flower shop.

We walked as fast as we could, half running to keep warm. A full, white moon shone in the inky sky, casting a silvery sheen across the snow. A shower came out of nowhere and with it a light wind that made the snowflakes dance and dip and turn in the streetlight glow like crazed mosquitoes.

"Rats," I said, putting up my umbrella. "I've brought that old paper umbrella with the tear. No wonder Otōsan got so wet in Tsurugi. The snow's coming straight through."

But I was lucky, and the shower stopped as suddenly as
it had begun. We skidded and slipped along icy footpaths,
past the night-lit shops of Korinbo. Turned left. The literature
museum's trees stood stark beneath their dusting of snow
powder. We passed the prefectural office, crossed the road, and
saw Aunt Yukiyo's melancholy Mr. Sawaguchi loom into view
in the dim light, drooping by the gate of Kenrokuen, ready to
open the gates to the lord's garden.

"Remember, this is a very special privilege. I wouldn't
do this for anybody in Kanazawa except your aunt. Be very
careful. No damage. You have one hour. I'll be waiting for you
here. Will you," he said, looking straight at me, "be all right
this time?"

I nodded. "No problems, Mr. S." I hoped there wouldn't be.

We hurried up the gravel slope past the empty ticket
booth. Even in the half light I could see how beautiful the
garden was, feel the power of its twelve thousand trees. A
green waterfall splashed winter music into an icy pond where
ducks were swimming. A flock of little grey birds with yellow
beaks, feeding on snow-strewn moss on the pond's opposite
bank, took flight when they saw us, swooshing over our heads
with a frenzied, frightened squawking.

It was slippery underfoot and my feet were freezing inside
Okaasan's rubber boots. We hurried past the Moonflower
Pavilion, across a bridge, and climbed a flight of steps. The
steps led on to a wide, gravel path where the light was a little

brighter. We trod fresh footprints across clean snow and climbed a slope. I could hear myself puffing.

Ahead I could see a fork in the path. We paused in the shadows of ebony-trunked trees and shivered as a small cold breeze was born. Snow lay thick along branches and on the stone lanterns. To our left it was banked on the roofs of the shuttered souvenir shops.

"The only dragon in Kenrokuen is the Dragon Rock," said Hiro. "It's a charm against evil spirits. It's just a bit farther. We go straight ahead and across the bridge."

It was the Rainbow Bridge, the one that shone red after rain. I'd read about it. Kanazawa's famous Kotoji Lantern stood beside it. I'd seen pictures of them heaps of times on postcards in the shops, so I stopped for a second to look, and to catch my breath. A frozen lake spread away from the bridge like a giant bed sheet, pines and bare cherries stark white in the snow along its banks.

"Come ON, Hannah! We can come back another time to look."

Miki's voice was urgent. Her eyes were shining with excitement. Hiro looked expectant in a calm kind of way. Me, I was beginning to wonder what we'd find when we reached the Dragon Rock. What if the dragon didn't like being woken up?

We veered right over another bridge and walked along the edge of the Misty Lake. Where the lake ended we turned left and followed a waterway. Hiro was looking carefully to each side of the path. A short distance along he stopped and pointed.

"That's it."

It was not one but a circle of rocks, odd mossy shapes hugging the ground. They formed a small coiled dragon with its wide mouth gaping. Deep green snow-scattered moss and fresh foresty vines covered its old head. Inside the coil of its body a black pine grew beside a stone lantern, and an azalea tumbled pink petals onto the moss and the snow. I looked up. Above us the sky had lightened to pale grey. A few pink clouds drifted across it. Day was coming. We had to hurry.

"Hiro, what's wrong? WHAT'S WRONG?"

I jumped at the panic in Miki's voice. She was staring in horror. I soon saw why.

"What?" Hiro looked blank.

"Your BREATH!!"

"Wow," said Hiro, crossing his eyes.

Miki and I were breathing the white misty breath of early morning. Hiro's breath was crimson.

"Hiro, are you okay?"

"Of course," answered Hiro. "But red means danger. 'Beware the one who does not want the boy to go.' Look!"

A flickering light was coming towards us through the stand of red pines behind the Dragon Rock. And behind the light prowled a figure all in white. I recognized the sleeve lantern before I saw the thin, sharp-eyed woman of Sarumaru Jinja. Her black hair was tumbled around her shoulders. She halted at the edge of the trees, fixed me with her crazy, mesmeric stare, spoke in the grating, whiny voice I remembered.

"You will not take him, foreigner. I cared for him from babyhood and he is mine. His mother died and left him, and I loved him. The woman of the snow is not here to help you, and you will not succeed. Do not dare to try."

Venom glinted in her sword-tip eyes. She swayed forward, drifting towards us. I couldn't move. When Hiro stepped into her path, she was so close I could already feel the cold spite of her being.

Hiro hadn't seen her in action at Sarumaru Jinja, but I still thought he was really brave to do what he did. Especially after the shock of having his breath turn red. He must have been shaking inside, but his voice was quiet and firm, and when he spoke he seemed much older than twelve.

"Why have you come here?" he asked.

She froze. Only the stony eyes moved, examining Hiro. Then suddenly, like a snake uncoiling, she bent towards him, bringing her lantern close to his face. "Do not question my presence, little spy. The child belongs with me, not with them."

Hiro edged backwards, closer to Miki and me. He was still puffing red smoke, blowing it out really fast. I suppose because he was scared. His voice was a bit wobbly. "Them?" he said. "Who are they? Who is waiting for Kai?"

She seemed to grow taller then, a stark black and white menace in the grey morning. "The father." She spat out the words. "The father waits. He who accused me. He will wait in vain." She smiled, sly and smug. Hiro was leaning close to me now, and I felt the muscles in his shoulder tighten. With fright, I thought. But when he spoke, his quiet voice was shaking with anger.

"Kai must go to his father. Children should be with their parents."

Her dentist-drill voice cut the air like a sword, but underneath her sharpness I sensed something uncertain. "I was his parent. I cared for him. I loved him."

"If you loved him, let him go to his family."

"Never. He is mine. Who are you to tell me what to do?"

"I am a boy," said Hiro softly, "who misses his father."

She sneered, took a step towards Hiro, an evil expression on her face.

"The rock," yelled Miki. "It's a charm against evil. Run for it."

We all tumbled for the Dragon Rock. The woman sped to reach it first. I fell down in the snow and clutched its head. Hiro reached a hand to its spine. Miki took a flying leap forwards, and as she did Auntie Frog Fetcher's jar of herbs rolled out of her pocket and on to the snow. Out of reach. The woman, her face alight with triumph, bent to take it.

"No!" Miki's voice rang high through the morning. At the same moment the first rays of sun broke through the clouds.

The woman froze. "Not the light," she whispered. "Not now."

She dropped the lantern on the path and the candle snuffed out. "I am forsaken."

Barely a whisper. Her shoulders sagged as she turned back to the trees. Breathless, we watched her fade slowly into the sun's rays, her white kimono mingling with the morning light until she was no longer there at all.

We had no time to lose. We picked ourselves up. Miki grabbed the jar, brushed off the snow and unscrewed the lid. "Let's hope this is right," she muttered.

We each took a handful of herbs and when Miki said, "Go," we scattered them over the Dragon Rock. At once a warm summer fragrance drifted into the wintry air. The earth gave a little shake, like an animal waking after hibernation, and from inside the dragon circle came creaking and puffing sounds. Lazy puffs of pink smoke popped from the azalea petals. The rocks shifted such a very little bit that you'd hardly notice. A crusty, grey body stretched. The dragon shut its red mouth, shook its green mane, turned its old head. Drowsy, amber eyes examined us.

"Good morning," it said courteously. "I daresay you've come about the boy. I knew the going was planned for today, but I wasn't sure if he'd make it. There was a peculiar woman hanging around. But no time to waste. Let's have the winter words, shall we?"

Miki cleared her throat. "*Yawarakai*."

"*Amai*," said Hiro.

"*Suppai*," I went last.

"Good grief," said the dragon, waggling his head. "Why are you talking about food? Tell me your winter poems and let's get on with it. I must hear *haiku* first thing in the morning. I can't wake up well enough to fly unless I hear beautiful *haiku*. I'm sure you have something nice for me. You first."

The dragon waggled its head in Miki's direction.

"Now we're in trouble," I whispered to Hiro. "He wants BEAUTIFUL *haiku*!"

"No talking," said the dragon.

Miki put her hands behind her back and carefully recited the *haiku* she'd written in the House of Cards. I knew we were in trouble the minute I heard it.

Basketball is fun
I want to win the next match
I love basketball.

The dragon got straight to the point. "That's ghastly," he said. "That isn't going to unfold my wings. How about you, the short one?"

"Mine's not very good either," I said hesitantly.

"Have a shot," said the dragon. "You never know your luck."

I stepped forward and bowed.

I beat Kenjiro
I want to whack him again
Harder and harder.

The dragon closed his stony eyes as if it couldn't bear to look at me.

"I see it IS possible to hear something more horrible than the basketballer's effort," he remarked. "I don't care for violent sentiments. There'll be no flying this morning if this goes on. Let's try you, boy. Have you got some beautiful winter words for me?"

Hiro glanced at Miki and me, and went red.

"Not shy, are you, boy? Don't worry about those two. They're talentless. Yours really couldn't be worse. Let's hope it's better."

The dragon looked smug, as if he was actually quite sure that Hiro's would be much, MUCH worse.

Hiro took an audible breath.

He left us in spring
Took flight to a secret place
Winter in my heart.

"Oooh," said the dragon, sounding like Otōsan. "Oooh, what beautiful winter words. How tragic. Such feeling. That's what I call poetry."

He shook his head at Miki and me. "You two should get some help. You're poetically disadvantaged. Yours was dreadful stuff. Ghastly. The boy's got talent, fortunately for you. He has given me energy and stamina, more than enough for a morning flight. The beauty of words is my nourishment, you know. Stand back now."

The sun was growing stronger. Its yellow light struck the grey rocks and the dragon, like a chameleon, transformed its body color to match. Grey to pink, pink to red, red to gold. It stretched again, fleshier now, sinuous and gleaming, and unfolded webbed wings, great, gauzy triangles shot with gold. Turning its glowing head towards us, it pointed a claw. "I'll be needing that red umbrella," it said. "Can't fly without a brolly. It may be a beautiful morning, but a snow storm's coming. A bad one. You'll see. Give."

"This umbrella? But it's got a big tear in it."

"Of course. How did you expect I'd carry the boy? On my back? A tear in an umbrella is designed to hide a soul. I don't want to be unkind, but you girls seem really stupid."

I handed the parasol over, feeling silly.

Miki recovered first. "Excuse me, um … Great Dragon, but how will you be helping Kai?"

"SO many questions!" sighed the dragon. "I will take his spirit to run with the sea and scatter the clouds. I will take him to the shelter of those who loved him, to the places where he was happiest. To his father and his mother. They've been waiting a long, long time. There's an uncle, too, I believe, who was very fond of him. All clear, missy?"

I had to ask. "Couldn't we see Kai just once before he goes? Because we sort of feel like we know him."

"See him? Can't help you there. Seeing ghosts is a gift.

And you lot don't have it, which I have to say doesn't surprise me, considering your lack of ability in other areas. Give me a little room, please. It's time to go."

We stepped back and the dragon lifted his wings and rose straight up like a helicopter above the tips of the red pines, the parasol open and clutched in a claw, whirling in circles like a red propeller. The sun rose in a burst above the snow and turned the waterway gold. Its glare blinded us and for a moment we couldn't see. Then, from out of nowhere, a Chocolate Surprise came spinning downwards and landed, splat, with a shower of chocolate syrup on the side of my face.

None of us spoke as we walked back to the entrance. Mr. Sawaguchi was waiting anxiously. In daylight he didn't look so damp. "Everything go all right?"

"Perfect, thanks, Mr. S." said Miki. "Aunt says you're to come for donuts very soon. Bring your friends."

Mr. Sawaguchi bowed wet gratitude and drooped away.

Then we all began to talk at once.

"That was SO amazing ... What you did was really courageous, Hiro ... Can you BELIEVE how rude that dragon was about my *haiku*? ... Do you think Kai is with his parents now? ... Won't they cry when they see him! ... Ghosts don't cry, Miki ... How do you know? They might ... He must have been so lonely all this time! ... If Miki hadn't found the message ... If Hannah hadn't come to Kanazawa ..."

"But I think he'll be okay now," said Hiro.

The little silver pavement holes were spitting out water, melting the snow and making it sloshy underfoot. We walked slowly through the rush hour crowds of people hurrying to their offices, past the Chinese restaurant and the coffee houses, past *sushi* bars with their window displays of plastic food and craft shops with their pottery and lacquer wares.

"What are you planning to do with this?" asked Hiro. He was carrying the sleeve lantern with his hankie wrapped around its stick so he didn't have to touch it.

"That will have to go to Otōsan for the Old Corner, don't you think?"

A papery gift might make it up to Otōsan, a bit, for all his trauma.

There was one more thing I wanted to do.

"After breakfast," I said, "I'm going to ask Otōsan if I can look at the books in the Old Corner, especially the ones that came with the yellow box. I can't leave things like this. I need to know more about Kai. I wish we could have seen him just once. And school reopens tomorrow, so after today there'll be no time. Don't you both think there must be a clue somewhere in the Old Corner? So will you help me? After breakfast? I'd do it by myself, but I only know fifty *kanji*!"

文

Chapter Twenty-Two

We began our search after breakfast, sitting on the floor of the Old Corner under the lantern. The Smoking Samurai was back from the living room. Otōsan, who was happy to have the samurai in the shop now he'd given up smoking, lifted the seven books that had come in the yellow box down from the shelves. We turned the pages slowly, careful not to damage their fragile paper. I was convinced we'd find a clue to Kai's story.

The first one was an account book, the second, an early twentieth century diary with only five entries. Miki read the entries aloud but they made no mention of ships or small boys. And besides, the early twentieth century was much too late for Kai. The Edo Period ended in 1867.

The third book was an eighteenth century novel. We could see the fourth was much older than the others, but it turned out to be the story of *Momotaro the Peach Boy*. Five was a volume of poetry. Six and seven were novels published in the 1960s. Nothing!

I hate the disappointment that comes when you're sure in your bones that something will go right and then it goes wrong. It gives me the heebie jeebies.

"We must be looking in the wrong place," said Miki.

"Maybe there isn't any right place to look," said Hiro.

But I wasn't giving up so easily. "There has to be a clue somewhere," I said. "I need to know who Kai was, and I'm certain we can find out if we just keep looking. Maybe we should check the other books."

"Dad's got hundreds," wailed Miki.

"Stupid!" said Hiro suddenly.

"Who?" Miki's voice was indignant.

"Me." He put the book he was holding back on the shelf. "Why don't we ask Professor Kato? He sent the yellow box. He might know something."

Miki jumped to her feet. "Of course. Let's phone him, Dad."

Otōsan shook his head. "Can't be done. He and his wife have gone to Sapporo for the Snow Festival and they're staying on to ski."

"Boring!" said Miki.

The house door opened and Granny pottered in with her donuts and took up her spot on the blue chair. Ten o'clock already. The fine weather of early morning had vanished.

Otōsan unlocked the shop door on to a night-dark day with snow gusting down, tossed in the teeth of a strong wind. Thunder rolled. Another storm was coming.

"*Buri okoshi*," said Hiro absently.

Miki wandered around the Old Corner, straightening masks. She shook the tail of a kite, ran one finger across the samurai's breastplate. "Let's walk to the 7-Eleven and buy ice cream," she said. "Ice cream helps me think."

"Eh?" said Otōsan. "Ice cream? Ice cream in this weather? No, no, Miki *chan*. Besides, you aren't walking anywhere in this storm. I don't like the look of it."

He slid the street door open a crack to have a look out. In the same instant a huge wind pushed the door wide and gusted in. Granny looked up and said, "Eh?" and took a good grip on her donut box.

The freak wind drove into every corner of the shop like a crazed demon. Greeting cards with their red and gold ties flew out of the card stand and into the air. Pencils rolled from shelves and clattered to the floor, and a stack of loose envelopes whooshed in aerobatic circles. The Old Corner frogs went spinning from their silk and the paper cranes flew into the air. The centipede kite waggled its tongue and slapped against the wall, and the masks rustled and shuddered. Five little paper lanterns blew off their hooks and floated to the floor. The small window above the Old Corner burst open, snow cascading in. And suddenly I knew why the scene was familiar. I was looking at the picture I'd seen in my dream, on my first night in Kanazawa. But something was missing. In the dream there'd been something else. Pages that someone had written on. Pages from a diary.

The orange lantern swung its light crazily, back and forth, back and forth, across the swirling paper, across the walls and along the lines of books in the shelves of the Old Corner, catching the shimmery gold of the samurai's helmet. Lightning flashed yellow through the shop, causing shadows like giant waves to roll across the walls. Boom crash smash, shouted the thunder. Hiro went running past me to shut the Old Corner window, ducked to avoid the flapping centipede, and bumped the samurai. The armor toppled over, hitting the floor with a loud clang, scattering the yellowed handwritten pages that had been hidden in its left gauntlet.

The wind died as suddenly as it had begun. The storm was passing, the rolling of thunder muted, distant. Snow drifted in gentle gusts through the shop door and Otōsan hurried to shut it. Hiro pushed the Old Corner window shut and Miki got a rag to mop up the floor.

Granny sat upright on her blue chair. "That was a surprise," she remarked.

I raced to the scattered armor and collected the pages, drying off their wet edges on the hem of my sweatshirt.

"Careful, Hannah," said Otōsan, coming over. "You don't want to damage the writing."

He could never resist old paper. He thumbed slowly through the pages, his expression turning to slow wonder under the floppy bangs. He looked up at us and beamed.

"Pages from a personal diary," he said, "belonging to Yoshi Kato of the Kato samurai family. Born 1813."

Edo Year 240 (1840)
The month of May

The events of the past year have been strange and disturbing and I feel compelled to write of them. Now we are in late spring and the sun warms my bones and the beauty of the cherry blossoms eases my heartache. Now I can write of the great sadness that befell my family during the winter past.

My name is Yoshi Kato, second son of the Kato samurai family. I am a physician, and in my twenty-seventh year. Since childhood I have desired with all my heart to travel to the farthest corners of the earth. To that end I have for some years been in the employ of the great merchant of Kanaiwa, Zeniya Gohei. I speak the English and Russian tongues with some skill, so I am useful to him. My master is a man of great standing, a cultured man of extraordinary wealth. Such is his fame that the Maeda lords of Kaga have conferred samurai status upon him, although he was born of a lowly merchant family.

I sail with Gohei's line as ship's doctor. We voyage often to Osaka and to the islands of Kyushu and Hokkaido. And on occasion to destinations more secret. Against all laws of the government, my master practices Mitsu Yunyū, secret trade with foreign lands. The risks are considerable but the rewards are many. For one such as I, not the least reward is the acquisition of greater learning, knowledge of new medicinal herbs and modern ways to cure the sick.

At the end of November in the year of 1838, on a day of sun and crisp wind, I sailed south from Kanaiwa in the brig Umikaze. We were a crew of ten under the command of Captain Hosokawa. My master Gohei's instructions were clear. Upon reaching Honshu's southern tip we did not turn east for Osaka, but continued south. Our destination was Van Diemen's Land.

Never before had I visited that place. Van Diemen's Land lies to the south of the Great South Land, Terra Australis. By rumor and sailors' talk I knew it to be a prison colony, and a place of great violence. But the trade is good. The meats and oils of black whales and sperm whales are excellent and plentiful, fur seal skins are to be had, and the boat building timber, felled by men in irons, is second to none. The merchants of that island buy our salt and rice, our lanterns and tools, and the candles we fashion from their whale and seal oil.

Our outward voyage was without incident, being one of calm seas, fair skies and a good hand of luck. We sailed up the Tamar River and docked at Launceston town under the new moon of April. I will not tell of the weeks spent on that island. It is a beauteous place, but sad and tortured. By the end of June our business was completed and my heart gladdened as we sailed north, bound for home. But our homeward voyage was to be one I would long remember.

Hours out of Launceston a great storm came upon us, a wild gale such as I have never known in all my time at sea. We were blown off course by demon winds, the ship tossed like a paper dingy between blue-black waves taller than houses, swept farther and further northwest, into that place men call the Desperate Straits. My heart was heavy and full of fear. If by chance we did not die in the storm, I was certain we would be killed by the feral men who dwell on the many islands of that place.

That stretch of ocean in the strait between Van Diemen's Land and the colony of New South Wales has an evil reputation. Vicious creatures live secretly among its many islands — freebooters, convicts and ship's deserters. Once they were sealers, but most of the seals are slaughtered now and the men live by whatever means they find to hand. They come to the islands from the slums and prisons of the north and south, half alive, starved and desperate, doing whatever they must to survive. They come to find others of their kind. Kidnappers they are, too, preying on the black girls of the mainland tribes. Female children of eight or nine years are kidnapped and enslaved by these felons, made to fetch wood, hunt kangaroo, club seals, clean skins, and kill and salt mutton birds.

In the depths of this wild and desperate night we saw what appeared to be the lights of a ship bobbing safe at anchor. I urged the captain to sail towards the lights, but he refused me. He had heard tales that wreckers, too, inhabit these islands. Sometimes, on a night of wild storm, they creep up and down rocky cliffs with lanterns, to deceive the crews of distressed ships into believing a safe harbor is within reach. The villains watch while the ships are torn to pieces on the reef, watch as men drown. In the morning they gather their plunder. Hosokawa knew we would have little chance to save or defend ourselves in the darkness, if such an incident should occur. He chose to take his chances with the elements. I prepared to die.

But the ways of the gods are strange, and sometimes merciful. We rode out the night and survived, and by daybreak the storm had died. We found ourselves many miles off-course, and drifting in dangerous waters. Sand shoals built up beneath the sea in that strait, everywhere there were submerged rocks, and fierce riptides swept through from east and west. And the Umikaze was taking on water. Feral men or none, we had to beach to make repairs. With great caution the captain sailed towards a craggy island, at the edge of which we could see a small sandy beach strewn with the detritus of the storm. Beyond the beach only low scrub and stunted trees grew. Attackers could not approach us unawares in that place.

The day was a gloomy one, a grey morning and cold. But I was happy to be alive and on land. I wandered, as I waited for the crew to complete the repairs, a short way from the beach, in search of wild parsley or other herbs that might keep scurvy at bay on the long voyage home.

I smelled the fire before I saw it, a thin trickle of pungent smoke rising beyond a slope some twenty paces distant. Hackles rose on the back of my neck. I dropped to my belly and slithered forward to the top of the rise, hoping to discover the number of men gathered, and their kind. What I witnessed there was unforeseen.

A girl child sat by the fire. Her hair shone in that drab place like a beacon, flame-colored, loose around her shoulders. Her wrists and ankles were bound, her chin rested on her knees. She was huddled close to the tall man who lay on the grass beside her. No words passed between then. He looked white and ill, made no movement. One side of his face was bloodied and I judged him unconscious. It was clear the pair were prisoners. There was no sign of their captors, who must have been, by nature of the situation, the ferals of the island. I suspected they would not be far away. I had to make my escape quickly. Could not, for the sake of my companions, become embroiled in conflict.

I must have made a noise as I started to edge backwards, because the girl looked up, saw me and recoiled in fright. Then hope dawned in her eyes. I was transfixed for an instant by those eyes. Blue as the autumn sky in Kanazawa they were, blue as the silk of my love's finest kimono. The child whispered something, a few words. Her voice was husky and her accent strange and I could not hear. I did not want to hear. My instinct was to fly, to forget what I had seen.

"Help us."

I made a gesture of refusal with my hand, made as if to slide back down the slope.

"Help us, please."

Clearer. I hesitated, and my heart smote me. My resolution was lost. I could not look at such despair in the eyes of a little child and do nothing. I could not bear to think of how she might suffer if I left her there a prisoner. I must do for them what lay in my power.

Keeping low to the ground I went over the lip of the slope and into the hollow. I split their bonds with my knife. She and I shouldered the sick man, and half-carried, half-dragged him back to the beach. The captain was angry. I had known he would be. He did not want a sick foreigner aboard. We did not know what fever the man was carrying. We did not know if the pirates would pursue us out to sea. But Captain Hosokawa is a good man, a man of integrity. I vowed to take all responsibility, and in the end he did not deny my request. Two sailors carried the unconscious man on board and into my cabin. The child followed, white and silent. There was no woman on board to care for her. She would have to manage as best she could.

Our luck held. We were again at sea before we heard shouts and vile curses from the beach. They did not pursue us. I think their boat was not nearby – I had seen none near the beach.

Our intention was to sail north to the settlement of Port Jackson, and deliver the man and the girl into care. But the man's condition grew worse. His fever burnt him like fire. He grew weaker and wandered in his mind. Forty-eight hours after her rescue, the girl too contracted the ague. I feared both would die, and we had no time to linger. The year was racing onwards. The captain sailed north with the foreigners aboard. We would bury them at sea, he said. We must reach Kanaiwa before the winter.

As I tended my patients, I considered what would happen if by chance they did not die, if we returned with them to our home. Foreigners are forbidden to enter Japan and the penalty is death. A grave prospect. I gave the matter much thought.

As fate would have it, the girl did indeed grow strong. The man's condition improved too, although he was yet delicate and easily fatigued. To my sorrow his condition worsened suddenly, three weeks out of Kanaiwa. Perhaps it was due to the spell of cold weather, or the strain the fever had put on his heart. He died suddenly at dawn one October morning. It was then I conceived my plan, a plan I confided only to my captain.

I knew the ship's crew must, for their own safety, bear no knowledge of what I planned to do. We threw two bodies overboard, but only one was truly a corpse. The girl was hidden below deck. She was grief-stricken for the loss of her father and in truth was not difficult to conceal. She ate little and made no noise.

In mid-November, as autumn turned to winter, we docked in Kanaiwa. Upon completing the business of arrival, the captain and I went to speak with my master, Gohei. I confessed my actions and the reasons for them. Truly Gohei is a great and generous man. His English friends in China, he said, would help the girl. Without hesitation he promised safe passage for her as soon as it could be arranged. Until that time I must hide her well.

I sent the girl to be hidden in my brother's house in Kanazawa, until weather and circumstance permitted her escape. My older brother, Himikaze Kato, was, still is, a soldier in the Maeda army, an officer, stationed at Myoryuji, the place they call the Ninja Temple. His home lies close by. The girl from Van Diemen's Land had to stay hidden in the house at all times, but in the winter cold that was not such a hardship. And she had Kai for her friend.

191

My nephew Kai was born at sea one summer night seven years ago. My brother and his wife were journeying home from Osaka by ship when the child was birthed early. They named him for the Sea of Japan, on which he was born. The girl, Holly, was two or three years older than my nephew. We hid her in part of the house unknown to the servants, rooms that could be reached from Kai's nursery, through a concealed door. The two quickly became as brother and sister. They played together in the nursery rooms and on the stairs, running and hiding, learning each other's languages. Although in truth they did not seem to need many words, as is the wont of children. Kai taught her Go and Hanafuda, the game of the flower cards. Both loved sweets, and I brought them mochi cakes whenever I could. Kai gave Holly his flower cards for her own. She gave him her only possession, a flower button made of glass, which was sewn into the hem of her dress when I found her. I believe it to have been her mother's. The girl knew she must leave Kanazawa as soon as it could be arranged. She told Kai she would know him when they met again, if he gave her the glass flower.

As winter advanced, the little girl was in part healed of her grief, Kai being an exceptional companion, intelligent and full of mischief, but with a fine heart. I would trust him with my life. In truth that is what I did. Holly too had a courageous heart. We came to love her as our own and would gladly have kept her with us had the laws of our country permitted.

It was from the Kamogawa woman that trouble came. Since the death of his wife, my brother employed Kamogawa in the *care of his son. And she loved the boy, of that I am sure. Over the matter of the foreign child she was sworn to secrecy and was well paid to keep her tongue quiet. My brother assured me she could be trusted. But Kamogawa proved herself an ignorant fool. Holly frightened her. Perhaps she was jealous of Kai's affection for the girl. She became convinced that a devil looked at us through the girl's blue eyes. She said the child would bewitch us. She became obsessed with this devil nonsense, and so she started to talk. She said nothing specific, but hinted in the neighborhood that something in the Kato household was not as it should be, whispered of her fears, of bewitchments and possession. She aroused suspicion, drew attention to us, and we knew that we must speed Holly away for her own safety, for ours and for my master's.*

There was little time. My brother conceived a daring plan, a plan that involved terrible risk. It was our only chance. One February midnight he smuggled Holly up a secret stairway into Myoryuji. He took her to the center of the temple, to the well of stone from Tomuro Mountain. With great trepidation he lowered her into the well, terrified she would fall to her death, terrified of discovery. Only the Maeda lords are allowed that path.

The child too was desperately afraid, but her courage endured. Trembling, sweat pouring from her brow, she clung to the rope until she found the opening to the lord's tunnel in the well's wall. My brother watched her disappear into the dark. Kai, who had made his way earlier to the banks of the Sai River, slipped into the tunnel from the opposite end and found Holly huddled there.

193

He guided her out and, by a secret and devious road, he led her to a thick copse of pine trees in Kabuto Machi. There my horseman was waiting. He rode with her to Kanaiwa and she sailed for China at dawn. Our hearts were full of joy when news of her safe departure reached us.

A day later my brother's boy fell ill with an infection of the lungs. The night of the girl's escape was one of bitter cold. Kai had walked far and he was unlucky. On his way back to his father's house, a party of soldiers crossed his path. He was forced to wait some hours in the snow by the river before they moved on and he could pass. He returned home at dawn, shivering and fevered, pains in his head and throat.

The past winter was one of extraordinary bitterness. By mid-February the snow lay so deep we had to leave and enter our homes through second story windows. The child's health did not improve. I did not know how to help. I went to the temple to pray, I attended the boy, did all in my power, tried every medicine I knew. My master, Gohei, sent many gifts of food. But the winds blew ever colder and the snow came thicker. Kai would not take nourishment. He fretted in his fever, called again and again for Holly, clutching her glass flower in his hand and refusing to leave hold. The flower cards he had given her lay beside him on his sickbed. Holly had not taken them with her. The method of her escape allowed her no possessions, but in his fever the boy could not understand, thought she had refused his gift.

Kai died late in February, falling at the last into an easy sleep. Never again would he walk on the winter beaches at

Kanaiwa, never swim in the warm summer sea. My brother
was wretched, sadder that any human being I have seen. I held
great fears for his life and his sanity. He sat alone day upon day,
his fingers running over Kai's toys, as if to touch them would
bring his son back. The boy's spirit, he said, walked restless in the
house. I too was desolate, and wracked with guilt. But the spite
and small-mindedness of Kamogawa was most to blame. I am
told that even now, when months have passed, she goes often to
Sarumaru Shrine to pray for the foreign girl's downfall. But Holly
is gone to safety and Kai is dead. Kamogawa's evil intentions will
change nothing.

In the early spring, sick at heart, I made a journey. I had
heard tell of a wise man, one who dwelt in a forest near the
shrine of the White Mountain, beside a pool where old frogs live.
I went in search of this sage, hoping for speech with him, looking
for comfort for myself, peace for Kai, and an end to my brother's
grief. And I was lucky, for he was at home. Of all that passed
between us I will not write. Suffice to say I left the forest with a
lighter and more peaceful heart, and bearing a tonic of herbs for
my grieving brother.

One thing only I will record here. The holy man has the
gift of future seeing. He has promised me that when the time is
right our family will be whole again, that Kai will find peace,
through the agency of a person or persons unknown. I do not fully
understand his meaning, but I choose to trust him. These were his
words:

If you, finder, choose to help the ocean boy,
Wait for the first snowfall.
The flute player at the temple of secrets
has the fox light.
At the hour of the bull bring the light to the shrine
Where women go to poison the hearts of their rivals.
After the bean throwing
Take the talisman you receive
To the place where the old mountain god
waits in the forest.
With the gift and your winter words from
the house of cards
Go at sunrise to wake the dragon that
sleeps in the lord's garden.
But beware the one
Who does not want the boy to go.
And remember always:
Blue for safety, yellow is warning, red means danger.

These words I will write on a separate sheet of paper and place with Kai's possessions, ready for the finder when he comes. My diary pages must be hidden, but I will not destroy them. I cannot say how the recording of this story has eased my heartache. My brother's pain, too, is a little less. I am hopeful that time and the wise man's herbs will bring him healing.

文

Chapter Twenty-Three

Miki, Hiro and I took the bus on a Sunday afternoon two weeks later, out through the suburbs of Kanazawa and west towards Kanaiwa and the sea. Spring was coming and the snow had almost gone. Intermittent clouds wandered across the sky, teasing the sun, only half serious about making rain.

I'd phoned my dad the day after we found Yoshi Kato's letter. I had to know if Holly was related to us. It didn't seem possible that she couldn't be. I felt like I knew her inside out. And Kai had thought I was her, or she was me. Dad couldn't tell me much.

He said that Holly was a family name and that his forefathers had settled in Launceston in the 1800s. But he didn't know anything about a child lost in Bass Strait.

He'd check, he said. But I didn't really need him to check,

because somewhere in my bones I knew.

Rain spattered suddenly against the bus windows, silvery drops glinting in the sun.

"It's a fox wedding," said Miki.

"What's a fox wedding?"

"A sun shower is a sign that somewhere two foxes are getting married. Everything foxes do is tricky, so when they marry, they make sure it's sunny and rainy at the same time. But foxes don't belong in this story, do they, Hannah?"

"I hope not, Miki," I said. "I think we have enough tricky things in this story already.

Maybe there'll be a sun shower when your aunt marries KimiShimi in April."

Hiro was looking forward to Aunt Yukiyo's wedding. I think half the reason was that he so badly needed to be part of a family and family things. He was also excited about the food. I wondered if Grandpa Honda would wear his blue terrycloth hat to the wedding.

Kanaiwa was timeless and Sunday-silent, a small, grey-blue, cloudy town under a milky sky. We turned left at the bus depot and wandered up a long, narrow street of old, brown-shuttered houses. Pines and azaleas and budding plum blossom peeped over a temple wall. A tabby cat sauntered out of a street on our right, where brightly colored bunches of plastic flowers and balls hung from the eaves of aged shops. Tiny sparrows chittered between the new buds of a cherry tree, and everywhere was the clean smell of newly cut timber. We could have been in any century.

But at the end of this old, quiet street, a wall was blocking our way. A very high, very ugly aluminum wall separated us from the beach. And all along the bottom of the wall lay rubbish from our own century: cans and bottles and bits of paper scattered and strewn around.

Miki's hands went to her hips and her black eyes flashed. "Look at this ugliness!" she said, glaring at us. "Why is this wall here? How are we supposed to see the ocean? And what's all this mess?"

Hiro ran a hand over the wall. "I suppose it's protection from the winter winds and high seas. They can be savage here, maybe even bad enough to destroy the town."

"That may be true, Hiro," said Miki grandly, "but could you tell me what purpose the rubbish serves?"

Looking at the wall and the rubbish, I wondered if we'd come all this way for nothing. We'd wanted so much to see the beach where Kai walked, the ocean he was named for. I looked up and down the street, and noticed a gap in the wall further to our right. I walked towards it. The two sides of the gap were linked by a chain, but at least I could see through. Beyond the chain was a stretch of patchy brown grass about six meters wide. Like the fence line it was strewn with cans and bottles, bits of plastic, old cartons, broken buckets and Styrofoam boxes. Signs read: DANGER, NO ENTRY. We weren't allowed to go on the beach!

I looked past the scattered rubbish. On the far side of the grass, an old fence bordered brown sand. The beach was wide and beyond it was the Sea of Japan. It rolled in great glorious winter-blue waves, their rushing foam pristine white, gulls wheeling above its hushing and shushing.

I half heard Miki asking Hiro what she was supposed to do if she wanted to walk on the beach in winter. How dare the beach be too dangerous to walk on! Hiro said it was certainly a shame, but of course the local people would clean it all up before the children wanted to swim there in the summer. Miki pointed out it would be easier not to put the rubbish there at all because then it wouldn't need to be cleaned up. She was going to bring up the matter of clean beaches at the next meeting of the environment club.

I let their voices fade, stood watching the water roll.

The afternoon light was uncertain, pale sun mingling with a new misty rain. Another fox wedding. And I saw that despite the sign, someone was standing on the beach. In the strange light at the water's edge was a small sturdy boy, dressed in *hakama* and a short kimono, hair pulled back in a ponytail. He was barefoot, ankle deep in water, looking out to sea.

I felt the others' sudden silence, knew they were watching with me. Rain and salt smell and hushed lemon light cocooned us, and when the boy turned we were ready. We saw a pointed, cushiony face and long solemn eyes with curious tip-tilted corners. The front of his head was shaven.

I slipped my charm bracelet off my wrist. Kai watched me carefully. I held it out towards him, held it high so the blue-glass flower caught the rainy light. We barely breathed.

Kai watched the flower. Then he smiled and the afternoon lit up with his happiness. For just a moment we were caught, all four of us, in a place beyond time, until the rain came heavier, mistier, and he was gone behind it.

"We did it," whispered Miki. "We finished his story."

"And I think we made him happy," said Hiro.

It was five-thirty when we got back to Kabuto Machi. We were chatting to Grandpa Honda outside the flower shop, enjoying the scent of jonquils and narcissus floating on the evening air, when a pale green taxi whizzed around the corner, zoomed along the street at breakneck speed, and skidded to a halt outside the Mulberry Tree. My eyes nearly popped out of my head when I saw the driver's wild purple hair. My mother leapt out of the front seat, pirouetted across the space between us and enfolded me in a bear hug. I was so surprised I nearly choked.

"Hallo, darling. Just back for a flying visit. Hallo, Miki. Hallo, Grandpa Honda. This must be Hiro. I've brought someone to see him." She waved an airy hand towards the cab.

We all turned to look. A small, tired-looking woman was climbing out of the back seat. A man followed her, a man with long wild hair, a beard and a bemused expression. Almost everyone who meets my mother has a bemused expression, so that was nothing new. What was new was that, despite the hair and beard, the man looked exactly like Hiro.

A blur that was Hiro flew past us, yelling. "Otōsan. Otōsan. *Kaette kita.*"

"Jiro!" Grandpa Honda's voice choked as he rushed forward. "Jiro, you've come back to us."

Apparently, my mother had found Hiro's father.

The question was how. Okaasan made tea and we all sat at the living room table to hear her story, my mother beaming and extremely pleased with herself.

"I found him," she said, "in a pineapple field."

"What were YOU doing in a pineapple field?"

"What was HE doing in a pineapple field?"

My mother held up a commanding hand. "You all knew I was going to Okinawa Island to meet the woman with the tropical balcony? So I did that. And she told me about her friend with the drooping datsura ..."

"What's a ... ?"

"It's a tree. Don't INTERRUPT, Hannah. I flew south from Okinawa to Iriomote Island, to find the drooping datsura garden, but the day I went looking for it I got LOST, and ended up in a pineapple field with a water buffalo. I don't know WHERE that animal came from. I PROMISE you I didn't leave the gate open."

She paused for a sip of tea. The Maekawas were all gaping at her with their mouths open, except Aunt Yukiyo, who was laughing. This family didn't turn a hair when a ghost moved in, but Liana's adventures had them stunned. I, on the other hand, was accustomed to her adventures, having experienced them from birth, but I have to say even I was pretty surprised at this one.

"So there I was, ambushed by the water buffalo. I was wondering what I should do, because I don't know how water buffalo like to be treated, when, to my EVERLASTING astonishment, a HAIRY VAGRANT just POPPED out of the bushes and shooed it away. And within seconds, and DESPITE my state of shock, I realized I KNEW the vagrant's face, although I'd never seen it with a beard. Grandpa Honda had shown me family photos and told me Jiro's story that first night at dinner. So I KNEW I was looking at Hiro's dad."

"But where was he all that time?"

"Now THAT'S quite a story. When he finished his moth research on Yonaguni he decided to hire a boat and slip up to Iriomote Island. He wanted to see an Iriomote wildcat, because he never had. He didn't plan to stay long and he didn't tell anyone he was going.

He arrived on Iriomote at dusk and set off on foot. No one saw him go. The wildcats are very shy and he had to travel deep into the island's interior, into the mountains, which are covered in thick jungle. He was alone deep in the forest at night when he stepped on a habu. Such a POISONOUS snake. He woke up days later in a cave behind a great waterfall, to find himself very ill and in the care of a peculiar old shaman who'd saved his life. His backpack and papers were gone – he thinks he may have dropped them over a cliff when the snake bit him. He was ill for a long time and then the rains came and he couldn't get out. And when the rains stopped he still couldn't get out, because the shaman had decided to keep him. From what I hear, if a shaman decides to keep you, you're pretty much stuck. In any case, they couldn't talk to each other because the shaman spoke a dialect that poor Mr. Honda couldn't understand. It took him MONTHS to work out a way to escape, and it was FATE that he walked OUT of the forest and straight into ME. And do you know, that shaman lives in a cave behind a waterfall, surrounded by exotic palms, in the center of marvelous primeval forest. TRULY! I'm considering going back there and putting that shaman in my book. Just THINK of the CAPTION: 'SHAMAN'S GARDEN SHROUDED IN MYSTERY'."

I privately thought it was a wonder poor Mr. Honda hadn't gone running back to the shaman, who apparently was about to become even more peculiar, courtesy of a visit from Liana. I didn't think he'd want to keep HER!

"Anyway, I said to Jiro, 'Darling, never MIND the airfare money. I'd be MORE THAN HAPPY to pay. You MUST come home, your family misses you TERRIBLY.' So we got on a plane and HERE we ARE."

"How did you find Mrs. Honda?"

"Oh, that was EASY. I knew she drove a taxi at Komatsu Airport. When we landed I MADE ENQUIRIES and TRACKED HER DOWN. I put them both in the back seat of the cab and home we came."

I wondered how many distraught policemen, airport

staff and members of the general public were on the verge of nervous breakdowns as a result of the enquiries and the tracking down.

Liana was already moving on. "What's been happening here?" she asked. "Has Hannah been BEHAVING HERSELF, Kie? Is she working hard at school?"

I looked at the Maekawas and grinned.

"Of course I have, Mum. I've been going to school and learning *kanji* and doing correspondence lessons. And we've been to lots of different interesting places. And met some interesting people. Haven't we, Miki?"

"I want to hear EVERY DETAIL later, Hannah. My flight to Kyoto doesn't leave until tomorrow afternoon, so we've got HEAPS of time. But for now, will you all excuse me. Kie, do you mind? I MUST do my WASHING!"

Author's Note

This is a work of fiction but its setting is real.

Kanazawa lies on the west coast of Honshu, Japan's largest island. Kabuto Machi, where the Maekawas live, is based on Kazue Machi, a teahouse district in the city's north, but its geography is different. The shops mentioned exist in Kanazawa, but they are not all in one area of the city.

The Omicho Market, the Asano and Sai rivers, the Ninja Temple, Sarumaru Shrine, the Ishikawa-mon Gate of Kanazawa Castle, Katamachi, Korinbo, Kenrokuen and the Dragon rock, Mount Hakusan, Nomachi Station, Shirayama Hime Shrine, Tsurugi, Kaga Ichinomiya, Kanaiwa, Okinawa Island, Iriomote Island and Yonaguni Island are all real places. The white horse does stand in the precincts of Shirayama Hime Shrine, but the Frog Fetchers, their pond and their frogs are fictional. As far as I am aware, no festival is held in the street of the Ninja Temple.

- The flower cards (*hanafuda*) were introduced to Japan by the Dutch at the beginning of the Edo Period. The Dutch were the only Europeans allowed to trade with Japan, operating from a tiny island in Nagasaki Bay. Traders were not allowed to cross to the mainland.

- *Setsubun*, the bean throwing festival, is celebrated each year on the third or fourth of February at shrines and temples and in private homes.

- *San* is a polite suffix used after surnames or after first names. *Chan* is used after the first names of children or very close friends. It is never used after surnames. *Kun* is used after the surnames or first names of male colleagues, classmates and friends. At work, a superior may use it when speaking to a subordinate. *San*, *chan* and *kun* are never used after your own name.

- *Zōri* and *waraji*, sandals woven from rice straw, were popular traditional footwear from the twelfth to the sixteenth centuries. *Zōri* were worn with *kimono*, *waraji* by travelers. *Geta*, wooden clogs, became popular in the Edo Period but priests from Daijoji Temple in Kanazawa wear straw sandals even today for their Deep Winter Ascetic Practices (*Kanshugyō*).

- Zeniya Gohei (1773-1852) turned Edo Period Kanaiwa into a boom town through his skills as a sea trader. By 1827, when he was fifty-four, he was a top class merchant with a fleet of two hundred ships. He acquired enormous wealth, and received a new name and samurai status from the Kaga government. Although it was forbidden by the central government in Edo, he had much contact with foreign traders. Australian whaling vessels operated in the seas around Japan from the 1830s onwards. In 1831, a Captain Russell of Hobart, sailing in the *Lady Rowena*, was involved in a skirmish with the people of Atsukeshi, in Hokkaido. In 1850 the *Eamont*, also from Tasmania, was wrecked off the Hokkaido coast.

Gohei may have traveled to Tasmania himself and he almost certainly sent a deputy to purchase land for him in the Launceston area. In the 1880s a party of Japanese entertainers were taken sightseeing outside Launceston. They found a large stone carved in *hiragana*. The inscription stated that the land was owned by Zeniya Gohei.

Gohei's contact with foreigners was noted by the Kaga government but no action was taken for some years. He was eventually executed in prison at the age of seventy-nine, by orders of his Maeda lord, who feared that Gohei's foreign operations would come to the attention of the Bakufu government in Edo.

• Younger samurai sons often married into lower class (but wealthy) merchant families in order to survive, as their own families could not afford to support them. Yoshi Kato, as the younger son of a samurai family, would possibly have married the daughter of a merchant. In this case Yoshi would not have used the surname Kato, but would have adopted the merchant's surname, if he had one. I have kept Yoshi's surname as Kato for the sake of clarity.

• Iriomote is one of the Nansei Islands, known for their age-old folk dances, shamanistic rituals, ancient Shinto shrines and Buddhist temples. Ninety percent of the island is mountainous and covered in primeval jungle. There are no roads to the interior, only foot trails. Very heavy rains fall in May and June. Many of the islanders speak a dialect very different to standard Japanese and would find it hard to communicate with someone from mainland Japan. The island is home to the habu, an extremely poisonous nocturnal snake, and the Iriomote wildcat, which lives deep in the interior and is considered a living fossil.

None of the characters in this story is based on any person, living or dead.

Acknowledgements

Special thanks to Dr. Kumi Kato, who acted as advisor on Japanese culture for the novel. I am indebted to Kumi for her insight, her generosity of thought and time, her painstaking attention to detail and her enthusiasm for the story.

In Kanazawa, my thanks to Sonoko Matsuda who generously gave her time to read the manuscript and make sure it was Kanazawa*teki*, to Masayuki Higashi and Yasuko Higuchi for their generous assistance with research, and to Shoji Higuchi who showed me Sarumaru Jinja. Thanks to Mr. Arakawa of the Zenigo Museum in Kanaiwa and to Jim Kable of Yamaguchi Prefecture for information on Zeniya Gohei.

At Penguin, thanks to editor Sandy Webster for her clever suggestions, humor and drive for excellence, to Jane Godwin who rescued the manuscript from the slush pile and added the final touches, and to Debra Billson for the perfect cover and design *(Australian edition)*.

Sue Gough's encouragement and the time she gave to talk me through a first draft rewrite were much appreciated. Thanks to Robyn Sheahan-Bright for her support and advice.

Jennifer Collins read the really bad drafts, which was hugely helpful and very brave. Deslie Christensen, Yuriko McCarthy, Gael Letts and Makiko Murakami helped with research. Last, but by no means least, I would like to acknowledge the beauty and magic of Kanazawa in winter.

Although I used a number of books to research the novel, two stand out as being of special value: *Kanazawa, the other side of Japan*, by Ruth Stevens, Kanazawa Tourist Association; and *The Art of Japanese Paper*, by Dominique Busson, Terrail.